Win____ ____ard
A TODAY Sho____ ____of the Year
A *Booklist* Editors____

"LaCour's prose is graceful and gut-wrenching. . . . this book,
while at times devastating, is also about forgiveness and acceptance,
as one might hope from the title. *We Are Okay* is a quick read
that's hard to put down, but it's the kind of story that lingers long after."
—*New York Daily News*

"[An] exquisitely rendered novel about loneliness, grief and healing. . . .
a portrait of relationships that are believably fraught with secrets and
unspoken emotion, yet, at their core, caring and not so easily broken."
—*Chicago Tribune*

"A meditation on surviving grief, *We Are Okay* is short, poetic and
gorgeously written . . . . The power in this little book is in seeing
Marin come out on the other side of loss, able to appreciate a
beautiful yellow-glazed pottery bowl and other people's kindnesses.
The world LaCour creates is fragile but profoundly humane."
—*The New York Times Book Review*

This book is provided by the Summer @ Your Library
project, which is supported by the U.S. Institute of Museum
and Library Services under the provisions of the Library
Services and Technology Act, administered in California
by the State Librarian.

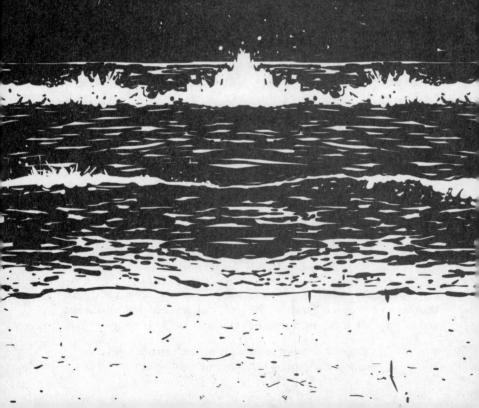

ALSO BY
Nina LaCour

Watch Over Me

Everything Leads to You

The Disenchantments

Hold Still

You Know Me Well
WITH DAVID LEVITHAN

WE ARE OKAY

a novel by

Nina LaCour

Penguin Books

Penguin Books
An imprint of Penguin Random House LLC, New York

First published in the United States of America by Dutton Books,
an imprint of Penguin Random House LLC, 2017
Published by Penguin Books, an imprint of Penguin Random House LLC, 2019

Visit us online at penguinrandomhouse.com

THE LIBRARY OF CONGRESS HAS CATALOGED THE DUTTON EDITION AS FOLLOWS:

Names: LaCour, Nina, author.
Title: We are okay : a novel / by Nina LaCour.
Description: New York : Dutton Books, an imprint of Penguin Random House LLC,
[2016] | Summary: "After picking up and leaving everything behind in
California, eighteen-year-old Marin, with the help of her former friend,
must confront her grief and the truths that caused her to flee her home"—
Provided by publisher.
Identifiers: LCCN 2016038096 | ISBN 9780525425892 (hardback)
Subjects: | CYAC: Loneliness—Fiction. | Orphans—Fiction. | Grief—Fiction.
| Grandfathers—Fiction. | Colleges and universities—Fiction. |
Lesbians—Fiction.
Classification: LCC PZ7.L13577 We 2016 | DDC [Fic]—dc23 LC record available at
https://lccn.loc.gov/2016038096

Penguin Books ISBN 9780142422939

Printed in the United States of America

20 19 18 17 16

Edited by Julie Strauss-Gabel

Designed by Anna Booth

Text set in Carre Noir

For Kristyn, more now than ever,

and in memory of my grandfather, Joseph LaCour,

forever in my heart

How and Why I Got Pretzel Dust in My Eyes
by Nicola Yoon

THIS IS THE STORY of how and why I got pretzel dust into my eyes.

It's a short story.

In the spring of 2017, I flew from Los Angeles to New York City for a book conference. It's a route I fly a lot, and I always take a few things to read with me. For this flight, I grabbed a copy of the gorgeous book you're now holding in your hands. I didn't know much about it, but I was already a fan of Nina's. I'd read *The Disenchantments*, Nina's beautiful story of heartbreak and band life. I'd also read *Everything Leads to You*, which is about secrets, second loves, and second chances.

As is my usual plane-reading ritual, I waited for the preflight announcements to be over, for the cabin light to be lowered, and for the seat belt sign to be turned off. Then I put on my headphones and settled in. From the first words, I knew this book was going to be special. Nina's prose is spare and joyous and fresh. Each sentence feels like something newly come to life. Beyond the beauty of the prose, though, is the profoundly moving depiction of Marin's journey from the raw loneliness of grief to a tentative and fragile hope for the future. Anyone who has experienced loss or heartbreak will find themselves in Marin and her story.

I don't remember much of what happened on the flight. Surely, I must have said yes to the flight attendant when he or she offered water and pretzels. It's possible I made room so that my seatmate could visit the restroom. All I remember from the flight is *We Are Okay*. How the book slipped quietly under my skin. How Nina's words built a small, glittering world of beauty and emotion and truth.

I came to the end of the book just as the flight began its descent into New York City. I could feel tears gathering inside me as I read the last words. To know me at all is to know that I'm a fairly shy and private person. I don't cry in public. But the seat belt sign was back on, so I couldn't get up and excuse myself to the restroom to have a good cry in private. I had no tissues except for the one cocktail napkin covered in pretzel dust. And I had a lot of tears—of joy and catharsis—that needed wiping.

So.

Now you know the story of how and why I got pretzel dust into my eyes.

This is a truly beautiful book. I loved it and I believe that you will, too.

—Nicola Yoon

WE ARE OKAY

chapter one

BEFORE HANNAH LEFT, she asked if I was sure I'd be okay. She had already waited an hour past when the doors were closed for winter break, until everyone but the custodians were gone. She had folded a load of laundry, written an email, searched her massive psychology textbook for answers to the final exam questions to see if she had gotten them right. She had run out of ways to fill time, so when I said, "Yes, I'll be fine," she had nothing left to do except try to believe me.

I helped her carry a bag downstairs. She gave me a hug, tight and official, and said, "We'll be back from my aunt's on the twenty-eighth. Take the train down and we'll go to shows."

I said yes, not knowing if I meant it. When I returned

to our room, I found she'd snuck a sealed envelope onto my pillow.

And now I'm alone in the building, staring at my name written in Hannah's pretty cursive, trying to not let this tiny object undo me.

I have a thing about envelopes, I guess. I don't want to open it. I don't really even want to touch it, but I keep telling myself that it will only be something nice. A Christmas card. Maybe with a special message inside, maybe with nothing but a signature. Whatever it is, it will be harmless.

The dorms are closed for the monthlong semester break, but my adviser helped me arrange to stay here. The administration wasn't happy about it. *Don't you have any family?* they kept asking. *What about friends you can stay with? This is where I live now,* I told them. *Where I will live until I graduate.* Eventually, they surrendered. A note from the Residential Services Manager appeared under my door a couple days ago, saying the groundskeeper would be here throughout the holiday, giving me his contact information. *Anything at all,* she wrote. *Contact him if you need anything at all.*

Things I need: The California sunshine. A more convincing smile.

Without everyone's voices, the TVs in their rooms, the faucets running and toilets flushing, the hums and dings of the microwaves, the footsteps and the doors slamming—without all of the sounds of living—this building is a new and strange place. I've been here for three months, but I hadn't noticed the sound of the heater until now.

It clicks on: a gust of warmth.

I'm alone tonight. Tomorrow, Mabel will arrive and stay for three days, and then I'll be alone again until the middle of January. "If *I* were spending a month alone," Hannah said yesterday, "I would start a meditation practice. It's clinically proven to lower blood pressure and boost brain activity. It even helps your immune system." A few minutes later she pulled a book out of her backpack. "I saw this in the bookstore the other day. You can read it first if you want."

She tossed it on my bed. An essay collection on solitude.

I know why she's afraid for me. I first appeared in this doorway two weeks after Gramps died. I stepped in—a stunned and feral stranger—and now I'm someone she knows, and I need to stay that way. For her *and* for me.

Only an hour in, and already the first temptation: the warmth of my blankets and bed, my pillows and the fake-fur throw Hannah's mom left here after a weekend visit. They're all saying, *Climb in. No one will know if you stay in bed all day. No one will know if you wear the same sweatpants for the entire month, if you eat every meal in front of television shows and use T-shirts as napkins. Go ahead and listen to that same song on repeat until its sound turns to nothing and you sleep the winter away.*

I only have Mabel's visit to get through, and then all this could be mine. I could scroll through Twitter until my vision blurs and then collapse on my bed like an Oscar Wilde character. I could score myself a bottle of whiskey (though I promised Gramps I wouldn't) and let it make me glow, let all the room's edges go soft, let the memories out of their cages.

Maybe I would hear him sing again, if all else went quiet.

But this is what Hannah's trying to save me from.

The collection of essays is indigo. Paperback. I open to the epigraph, a quote by Wendell Berry: "In the circle of the human we are weary with striving, and are without rest." My particular circle of the human has fled the biting cold for the houses of their parents, for crackling fireplaces or tropical destinations where they will pose in bikinis and Santa hats to wish their friends a Merry Christmas. I will do my best to trust Mr. Berry and see their absence as an opportunity.

The first essay is on nature, by a writer I've never heard of who spends pages describing a lake. For the first time in a long time, I relax into a description of setting. He describes ripples, the glint of light against water, tiny pebbles on the shore. He moves on to buoyancy and weightlessness; these are things I understand. I would brave the cold outside if I had a key to the indoor pool. If I could begin and end each day of this solitary month by swimming laps, I would feel so much better. But I can't. So I read on. He's suggesting that we think about nature as a way to be alone. He says lakes and forests reside in our minds. Close your eyes, he says, and go there.

I close my eyes. The heater clicks off. I wait to see what will fill me.

Slowly it comes: Sand. Beach grass and beach glass. Gulls and sanderlings. The sound and then—*faster*—the sight of waves crashing in, pulling back, disappearing into ocean and sky. I open my eyes. It's too much.

The moon is a bright sliver out my window. My desk lamp, shining on a piece of scratch paper, is the only light on in all one hundred rooms of this building. I'm making a list, for after Mabel leaves.

read the NYT *online each morning*
buy groceries
make soup
ride the bus to the shopping district/library/café
read about solitude
meditate
watch documentaries
listen to podcasts
find new music . . .

I fill the electric kettle in the bathroom sink and then make myself Top Ramen. While eating, I download an audiobook on meditation for beginners. I press play. My mind wanders.

Later, I try to sleep, but the thoughts keep coming. Everything's swirling together: Hannah, talking about meditation and Broadway shows. The groundskeeper, and if I will need something from him. Mabel, somehow arriving here, where I live now, somehow making herself a part of my life again. I don't even know how I will form the word *hello*. I don't know what I will do with my face: if I will be able to smile, or even if I should. And through all of this is the heater, clicking on and off, louder and louder the more tired I become.

I turn on my bedside lamp and pick up the book of essays.

I could try the exercise again and stay on solid ground this time. I remember redwood trees so monumental it took five of us, fully grown with arms outstretched, to encircle just one of them. Beneath the trees were ferns and flowers and damp, black dirt. But I don't trust my mind to stay in that redwood grove, and right now, outside and covered in snow, are trees I've never wrapped my arms around. In this place, my history only goes three months back. I'll start here.

I climb out of bed and pull a pair of sweats over my

leggings, a bulky sweater over my turtleneck. I drag my desk chair to my door, and then down the hall to the elevator, where I push the button for the top floor. Once the elevator doors open, I carry the chair to the huge, arched window of the tower, where it's always quiet, even when the dorm is full. There I sit with my palms on my knees, my feet flat on the carpet.

Outside is the moon, the contours of trees, the buildings of the campus, the lights that dot the path. All of this is my home now, and it will still be my home after Mabel leaves. I'm taking in the stillness of that, the sharp truth of it. My eyes are burning, my throat is tight. If only I had something to take the edge off the loneliness. If only *lonely* were a more accurate word. It should sound much less pretty. Better to face this now, though, so that it doesn't take me by surprise later, so that I don't find myself paralyzed and unable to feel my way back to myself.

I breathe in. I breathe out. I keep my eyes open to these new trees.

I know where I am, and what it means to be here. I know Mabel is coming tomorrow, whether I want her to or not. I know that I am always alone, even when surrounded by people, so I let the emptiness in.

The sky is the darkest blue, each star clear and bright. My palms are warm on my legs. There are many ways of being alone. That's something I know to be true. I breathe in (stars and sky). I breathe out (snow and trees).

There are many ways of being alone, and the last time wasn't like this.

Morning feels different.

I slept until almost ten, when I heard the groundskeeper's truck on the drive below my room, clearing the snow. I'm showered and dressed now; my window lets in daylight. I choose a playlist and plug Hannah's speakers into my computer. Soon an acoustic guitar strum fills the room, followed by a woman's voice. Electric kettle in hand, I prop open my door on the way to the bathroom sink. The song follows me around the corner. I leave the bathroom door open, too. As long as I'm their only inhabitant, I should make these spaces feel more like mine.

Water fills the kettle. I look at my reflection while I wait. I try to smile in the way I should when Mabel arrives. A smile that conveys as much welcome as regret. A smile with meaning behind it, one that says all I need to say to her so I don't have to form the right words. I shut off the faucet.

Back in my room, I plug in the kettle and pick up my yellow bowl from where it rests, tipped over to dry, from last night. I pour in granola and the rest of the milk from the tiny fridge wedged between Hannah's desk and mine. I'll be drinking my breakfast tea black this morning.

In seven and a half hours, Mabel will arrive. I cross to the doorway to see the room as she'll see it. Thankfully, Hannah's brought some color into it, but it only takes a moment to notice the contrast between her side and mine. Other than my plant and the bowls, even my desk is bare. I sold back all of last semester's textbooks two days ago, and I don't really want her to see the book on solitude. I slip it into my closet—there's plenty of room—and when I turn back, I'm faced with the worst part of all: my bulletin board without a single thing on it. I may not be able to do much about my smile, but I can do something about this.

I've been in enough other dorm rooms to know what to do. I've spent plenty of time looking at Hannah's wall. I need quotes from songs and books and celebrities. I need photographs and souvenirs, concert ticket stubs, evidences of inside jokes. Most of these are things I don't have, but I can do my best with pens and paper and the printer Hannah and I share. There's a song Hannah and I have been listening to in the mornings. I write the chorus from memory in purple pen, and then cut the paper in a square around the words.

I spend a long time online choosing a picture of the moon.

Keaton, who lives two doors down, has been teaching us all about crystals. She has a collection on her windowsill, always sparkling with light. I find the blog of a woman named Josephine who explains the healing properties of gemstones and how to use them. I find images of pyrite (for protection), hematite (for grounding), jade (for serenity). Our color printer clicks and whirrs.

I regret selling my textbooks back so soon. I had sticky notes and faint pencil scrawls on so many of the pages. In history we learned about the Arts and Crafts movement, and there were all these ideas I liked. I search for William Morris, read essay after essay, trying to find my favorite of his quotes. I copy a few of them down, using a different color pen for each. I print them out, too, in various fonts, in case they'll look better typed. I search for a redwood tree that resembles my memories and end up watching a mini-documentary on redwood ecosystems, in which I learn that during the summertime California redwoods gather most of their water from the fog, and that they provide homes to clouded salamanders, who have no lungs and breathe through their skin. I press print on a picture of a clouded salamander on bright green moss, and once the printer stops, I think I have enough.

I borrow a handful of Hannah's pushpins and arrange everything I've printed and written, and then step back and look. Everything is too crisp, too new. Each paper is the same white. It doesn't matter that the quotes are interesting and pictures are pretty. It looks desperate.

And now it's almost three already and I've wasted these

hours and it's becoming difficult to breathe because six thirty is no longer far in the future. Mabel knows me better than anyone else in the world, even though we haven't spoken at all in these four months. Most of her texts to me went unanswered until eventually she stopped sending them. I don't know how her Los Angeles life is. She doesn't know Hannah's name or what classes I've taken or if I've been sleeping. But she will only have to take one look at my face to know how I'm doing. I take everything off my bulletin board and carry the papers down the hall to the bathroom in the other wing, where I scatter them into the trash.

There will be no way to fool her.

The elevator doors open but I don't step inside.

I don't know why I've never worried about the elevators before. Now, in the daylight, so close to Mabel's arrival, I realize that if they were to break, if I were to get stuck inside alone, and if my phone weren't able to get service, and no one was on the other end of the call button, I would be trapped for a long time before the groundskeeper might think to check on me. Days, at least. Mabel would arrive and no one would let her in. She would pound at the door and not even I would hear her. Eventually, she would get back in her cab and wait at the airport until she found a flight to take her home.

She would think it was almost predictable. That I would disappoint her. That I would refuse to be seen.

So I watch as the doors close again and then I head to the stairs.

The cab I called waits outside, engine idling, and I make a crushed ice trail from the dorm lobby, thankful for Hannah's spare pair of boots, which are only a tiny bit small and which she forced on me when the first snow fell. ("You have *no idea*," she told me.)

The cab driver steps out to open my door. I nod my thanks.

"Where to?" he asks, once we're both inside with the heat going strong, breathing the stale cologne-and-coffee air.

"Stop and Shop," I say. My first words in twenty-four hours.

The fluorescent grocery-store lights, all the shoppers and their carts, the crying babies, the Christmas music—it would be too much if I didn't know exactly what to buy. But the shopping part is easy. Microwave popcorn with extra butter flavor. Thin stick pretzels. Milk chocolate truffles. Instant hot chocolate. Grapefruit-flavored sparkling water.

When I climb back into the cab, I have three heavy bags full of food, enough to last us a week even though she'll only be here three days.

The communal kitchen is on the second floor. I live on the third and I've never used it. I think of it as the place girls in clubs bake brownies for movie nights, or a gathering spot for groups of friends who feel like cooking an occasional dinner as a break from the dining hall. I open the refrigerator to discover it empty. It must have been cleaned out for the break. Instructions tell us to label all of our items with our initials, room number, and date. Even though I'm the only one here, I reach for the Sharpie and masking tape. Soon, food labeled as mine fills two of the three shelves.

Upstairs in my room, I assemble the snacks on Hannah's desk. It looks abundant, just as I'd hoped. And then my phone buzzes with a text.

I'm here.

It isn't even six o'clock yet—I should still have a half hour at least—and I can't help but torture myself by scrolling up to see all of the texts Mabel sent before this one. Asking if I'm okay. Saying she's thinking of me. Wondering where the fuck am I, whether I'm angry, if we can talk, if she can visit, if I miss her. *Remember Nebraska?* one of them says, a reference to a plan we never intended to keep. They go on and on, a series of unanswered messages that seize me with guilt, until I'm snapped out of it by the phone ringing in my hand.

I startle, answer it.

"Hey," she says. It's the first time I've heard her voice since everything happened. "I'm downstairs and it's fucking freezing. Let me in?"

And then I am at the lobby door. We are separated by only a sheet of glass and my shaking hand as I reach to turn the lock. I touch the metal and pause to look at her. She's blowing into her hands to warm them. She's faced away from me. And then she turns and our eyes meet and I don't know how I ever thought I'd be able to smile. I can barely turn the latch.

"I don't know how anyone can live anywhere this cold," she says as I pull open the door and she steps inside. It's freezing down here, too.

I say, "My room is warmer."

I reach for one of her bags carefully, so our fingers don't touch. I'm grateful for the weight of it as we ride the elevator up.

The walk down the hallway is silent and then we get to my door, and once inside she sets down her suitcase, shrugs off her coat.

Here is Mabel, in my room, three thousand miles away from what used to be home.

She sees the snacks I bought. Each one of them, something she loves.

"So," she says. "I guess it's okay that I came."

chapter two

MABEL IS FINALLY WARM ENOUGH. She tosses her hat onto Hannah's bed, unwraps her red-and-yellow scarf. I flinch at the familiarity of them. All of my clothes are new.

"I'd make you give me a tour, but there's no way I'm going back out there," she says.

"Yeah, sorry about that," I say, still fixed to her scarf and hat. Are they as soft as they used to be?

"You're apologizing for the weather?" Her eyebrows are raised, her tone is teasing, but when I can't think of anything witty to say back, her question hovers in the room, a reminder of the apology she's really come for.

Three thousand miles is a long way to travel to hear someone say she's sorry.

"So what are your professors like?"

Thankfully, I manage to tell her about my history

professor, who swears during lessons, rides a motorcycle, and seems much more like someone you'd meet at a bar than in a lecture hall. This topic doesn't make me a gifted conversationalist, but at least it makes me adequate.

"At first I kept thinking all my professors were celibate," I say. She laughs. *I made her laugh.* "But then I met this guy and he shattered the illusion."

"What building is his class in? We can do a window tour."

Her back is to me as she peers out at my school. I take a moment too long before joining her.

Mabel.

In New York. In my room.

Outside, the snow covers the ground and the benches, the hood of the groundskeeper's truck, and the trees. Lights on the pathways glow even though nobody's here. It looks even emptier this way. So much light and only stillness.

"Over there." I point across the night to the furthermost building, barely lit up.

"And where's your lit class?"

"Right here." I point to the building next to us.

"What else are you taking?"

I show her the gym where I swim laps every morning and try, unsuccessfully, to master the butterfly stroke. I swim late at night, too, but I don't tell her that. The pool is always eighty degrees. Diving in feels like plunging into nothing, not the icy shock I've known forever. No waves cold enough to numb me or strong enough to pull me under. At night the pool is quiet, and I swim laps and then just float, watching the ceiling or closing my eyes, all the sounds foggy and distant, the lifeguard keeping watch.

It helps me get calm when the panic starts.

But when it's too late at night and the pool is closed and I can't stop my thoughts, it's Hannah who can steady me.

"I just read the most interesting thing," she'll say from her bed, her textbook resting in her lap. And then she reads to me about honeybees, about deciduous trees, about evolution.

It takes me a while, usually, to be able to listen. But when I do, I discover the secrets of pollination, that honeybees' wings beat two hundred times per second. That trees shed their leaves not according to season, but according to rainfall. That before all of us there was something else. Eventually, something will take our place.

I learn that I am a tiny piece of a miraculous world.

I make myself understand, again, that I am in a dorm room at a college. That what happened has happened. It's over. Doubt pushes in, but I use our twin beds and desks and closets, the four walls around us, the girls who neighbor us on both sides and the ones who neighbor them, the whole building and the campus and the state of New York to fend doubt off.

We are what's real, I tell myself as I fall asleep.

Then, at six a.m., when the pool opens, I go swimming.

A movement calls me back. Mabel, tucking her hair behind her ear. "Where's the dining hall?" she asks.

"You can't see it from this window, but it's across the courtyard in the back."

"What's it like?"

"Decent."

"I mean the people. The scene."

"Pretty mellow. I usually sit with Hannah and her friends."

"Hannah?"

"My roommate. Do you see the building with the pointy roof? Behind those trees?"

She nods.

"That's where my anthropology class is. It's probably my favorite."

"Really? Not lit?"

I nod.

"Because of the professors?"

"No, they're both good," I say. "Everything in lit is just too . . . ambiguous, I guess."

"But that's what you like. All the differences in interpretation."

Is that true? I can't remember.

I shrug.

"But you're still an English major."

"No, I'm undeclared now," I say. "But I'm pretty sure I'm going to switch to Natural Sciences."

I think I see a flash of annoyance cross her face, but then she smiles at me.

"Bathroom?" she asks.

"Follow me."

I lead her around the corner, then return to my room.

Three days suddenly feels so long. Unfathomable, all the minutes Mabel and I will need to fill. But then I see her scarf on the bed, her hat next to it. I pick them up. They're even softer than I remembered and they smell like the rosewater Mabel and her mom spray everywhere. On themselves and in their cars. In all the bright rooms of their house.

I hold on to them and keep holding even when I hear Mabel's footsteps approach. I breathe in the rose, the earthiness of Mabel's skin, all the hours we spent in her house.

Three days will never be enough.

"I have to call my parents," Mabel says from the doorway. I set down her things. If she noticed me holding them, she isn't going to acknowledge it. "I texted them from the airport, but they're so nervous about this. They kept giving me tips about driving in the snow. I kept saying, 'I'm not going to be the one driving.'"

She puts her phone to her ear, but even from across the room I can hear when they answer, both Ana's voice and Javier's, exuberant and relieved.

The briefest fantasy: *Mabel appears at the doorway, catches sight of me. She sits next to me on the bed, takes the hat, and sets it down. Takes the scarf from my hands and wraps it around my neck. Takes my hands and warms them in hers.*

"Yes," she says, "the plane was fine. . . . I don't know, it was pretty big. . . . No, they didn't serve food."

She looks at me.

"Yes," she says. "Marin's right here."

Will they ask to talk to me?

"I have to go check on something," I tell her. "Say hi for me."

I slip out the door and down the stairs to the kitchen. I open the refrigerator. Everything is exactly as I left it, neatly labeled and arranged. We could make ravioli and garlic bread, quesadillas with beans and rice on the side, vegetable soup, a spinach salad with dried cranberries and blue cheese, or chili with corn bread.

I spend long enough away that by the time I get back Mabel has hung up.

chapter three

I SLEPT THROUGH MY ALARM, woke to Gramps singing to me from the living room. A song about a sailor dreaming, about Marin, his sailor girl. His accent was slight—he'd lived in San Francisco since he was nine—but when he sang, he became unmistakably Irish.

He tapped on my door, sang a verse loudly just outside.

Mine was the front bedroom, overlooking the street, while Gramps occupied two rooms in the back of the house. Between us were the living room and dining room and kitchen, so we could pretty much do whatever we wanted without fear that the other would be listening. He never came into my room; I never went into his. That might sound unfriendly, but it wasn't. We spent plenty of time together in the in-between rooms, reading on the sofa and the easy chair; playing cards in the dining room; cooking together;

eating at the round kitchen table, so small that we never had to ask the other to pass the salt and our knees bumped so often we didn't bother apologizing. Our hampers were in the hall by the bathroom and we took turns doing laundry, leaving neatly folded stacks on the dining room table for the other to take whenever the time was right. Maybe parents or spouses would have taken the clothes and opened up the other one's drawers, but we were not father and daughter. We were not spouses. And in our house, we enjoyed our togetherness but we enjoyed our apartness, too.

His song trailed off as I opened my door to his wide-knuckled, age-spotted hand, holding out coffee in the yellow mug. "You'll need a ride today. And from the looks of you, you'll need this coffee." Yellow morning light, beating through the curtains. Blond hair in my eyes until I pushed it away.

A few minutes later we were in the car. The news was all about a prisoner of war who had been brought back, and Gramps kept saying, "What a shame. Such a young boy," and I was glad he had something to engage himself because I was thinking about last night.

About Mabel and all of our other friends, cross-legged in the sand, part shadowed, part lit in the bonfire glow. It was May already. We'd all be leaving one another, going to other places in the fall; and now that the season was changing, rushing toward graduation, everything we did felt like a long good-bye or a premature reunion. We were nostalgic for a time that wasn't yet over.

"So young," Gramps was saying. "To endure a thing like that. And people can be so heartless."

He set his blinker on as we approached the drop-off zone at Convent. I held my coffee cup out so it wouldn't slosh as he turned.

"Look at that," he said, pointing at the dashboard clock. "Two minutes to spare."

"You're my hero," I told him.

"You be good," he said. "And careful—don't let the sisters know we're heathens."

He grinned. I took my last sips.

"I won't."

"Take an extra helping of the blood of Christ for me, will you?"

I rolled my eyes, set my empty mug on the seat.

I shut the door and leaned down to wave at him, still delighted by his own jokes, through the rolled-up window. He made his face fake-somber and crossed himself before laughing and driving away.

In English, we were talking about ghosts. About whether they were there at all, and if they were, whether they were as evil as the governess in *The Turn of the Screw* thought.

"Here are two statements," Sister Josephine said. "One:

The governess is hallucinating. Two: The ghosts are real."
She turned and wrote both on the board. "Find evidence
in the novel for both of these. Tomorrow, we'll discuss as a
class."

My hand shot up. "I have a third idea."

"Oh?"

"The staff is conspiring against her. An elaborate trick."

Sister Josephine smiled. "Intriguing theory."

Mabel said, "It's complicated enough with two," and a
few other people agreed with her.

"It's better if it's complicated," I said.

Mabel turned in her desk to face me. "Wait. Excuse me?
It's *better* if it's *complicated*?"

"Of course it is! It's the point of the novel. We can search
for the truth, we can convince ourselves of whatever we want
to believe, but we'll never actually know. I *guarantee* that we
can find evidence to argue that the staff is playing a trick on
the governess."

Sister Josephine said, "I'll add it to the list."

After school, Mabel and I split up our science assignment on
the 31, hopped off around the corner from Trouble Coffee,
and went in to celebrate our excellent time management
with two cappuccinos.

"I keep thinking about ghosts," I said as we walked

alongside the pastel houses with flat façades and square windows. "They show up in all my favorite books."

"Final essay topic?"

I nodded. "But I have to figure out a thesis."

"The only thing I like about *The Turn of the Screw* is the governess's first sentence." Mabel paused to tug on her sandal strap.

I closed my eyes and felt the sun on my face. I said, "'I remember the whole beginning as a succession of flights and drops, a little seesaw of the right throbs and the wrong.'"

"Of *course* you would know it by heart."

"Well, it's amazing."

"I thought the whole thing would be that way, but it's just confusing and pointless. The ghosts—if there *are* ghosts—don't even do anything. They just show up and stand around."

I opened our iron gate and we climbed the stairs to the landing. Gramps was calling hello before we'd even closed the door behind us. We set down our coffees, shrugged off our backpacks, and went straight to the kitchen. His hands were covered in flour; Wednesdays were his favorite because there were two of us to bake for.

"Smells delicious," Mabel said.

"Say it in Spanish," Gramps said.

"*Huele delicioso*. What is it?" Mabel said.

"Chocolate Bundt cake. Now say, 'The chocolate Bundt cake smells delicious.'"

"Gramps," I said. "You're exoticizing her again."

He lifted his hands, busted. "I can't help it if I want to hear some words in a beautiful language."

She laughed and said the sentence, and many other sentences with only a few words I understood, and Gramps wiped his hands on his apron and then touched them to his heart.

"Beautiful!" he said. "*Hermosa!*"

And then he headed out of the kitchen and saw something that made him stop. "Girls. Please sit."

"Uh-oh. The love seat," Mabel whispered.

We crossed to the faded red love seat and sat together, waiting to discover the subject of that afternoon's lecture.

"Girls," he said again. "We have to talk about *this*." He picked up one of the to-go cups that we'd set on the coffee table, held it with disdain. "When I was growing up, none of this stuff was here. *Trouble Coffee*. Who names an establishment 'Trouble'? A bar, sure, maybe. But a café? No. Mabel's parents and I spend good money to send you girls to a nice school. Now you want to stand in lines to buy lunch and spend far too much on a cup of coffee. How much did this cost?"

"Four dollars," I said.

"*Four? Each?*" He shook his head. "Let me offer you a

helpful piece of advice. That is three dollars more than a cup of coffee should be."

"It's a cappuccino."

He sniffed the cup. "They can call it whatever they want to call it. I have a perfectly good pot in the kitchen and some beans that are fresh enough for anyone."

I rolled my eyes, but Mabel was ardent in her respect for elders.

"It was a splurge," she said. "But you're right."

"*Four* dollars."

"Come on, Gramps. I smell the cake. Shouldn't you check on it?"

"You're a sly girl," he said to me.

"No," I said. "Only hungry."

And I was. It was torture to wait for the cake to cool, but when it did, we devoured it.

"Save a sliver for the fellas!" Gramps implored us, but for four old guys, his friends were the pickiest eaters I'd ever known. Like the girls at school, they were off gluten one week only to suddenly be on it again if the meal was enticing enough. They were laying off sugar or carbs or caffeine or meat or dairy, but maybe a little butter was fine now and then. When they broke their own rules, they complained about it. Took bites of Gramps's sweets and declared them too sugary.

"They don't deserve this cake," I said between bites.

"They won't appreciate it like we do. Maybe you should mail a piece to Birdie. Overnight it."

"Does she know about your baking?" Mabel asked him.

"I may have mentioned it once or twice."

"One bite of this and she'll be yours forever," Mabel said.

Gramps shook his head and laughed, and Mabel and I were soon stuffed and happy, traipsing back out as Jones, the first of Gramps's buddies, arrived, holding his lucky card deck in one hand and his cane in the other.

I took a minute to talk to him.

"Agnes is having surgery on her hand again Tuesday," he told me.

"Do you guys need any help with anything?"

"Samantha's taking some days off from the salon," he said.

"Maybe I'll come by and say hi."

Samantha was Jones and Agnes's daughter, and she'd been so nice to me in the months I lived with them when I was eight and Gramps had to spend some time in the hospital. She drove me to school and back every day, and even after Gramps came home she helped us, picking up his new prescriptions and making sure we had food in the house.

"She'd love to see you."

"All right," I said. "We're headed to the beach. Try to hold on to your money."

Mabel and I walked the four blocks to the beach. We slipped off our sandals where the road met the sand and carried them up a dune, weaving through patches of beach grass and the green-and-rust-colored ice plants. We sat at a safe distance from the water while the flocks of gray-and-white sanderlings pecked at the shore. At first it looked like no one was out there, but I knew to watch and to wait, and soon, I saw them: a pair of surfers in the distance, now mounting their boards to catch a wave. We watched them against the horizon line, rising and falling. An hour passed, and we lost sight of them over and over, and each time found them again.

"I'm cold," Mabel said when the fog set in.

I scooted closer to her until the sides of our bodies touched. She gave me her hands, and I rubbed them until we were warm. She wanted to go home, but the surfers were still in the water. We stayed until they reached the sand, tucked their boards under their arms, turquoise and gold against their wet suits. I waited to see if one of them would know me.

They got closer, a man and a woman, both squinting to see if I was who they thought I'd be.

"Hey, Marin," the man said.

I lifted my hand.

"Marin, I have something for you." The woman unzipped

her backpack and pulled out a shell. "Claire's favorite kind," she said, pressing it into my palm.

Then they were past us, making their way to the parking lot.

"You haven't asked me what I'm writing about," Mabel said.

The shell was wide and pink, covered in ridges. Dozens like it filled three large mason jars in my bedroom, all of them gifts. She held out her hand and I dropped it in.

"Jane Eyre. Flora and Miles. Basically everyone in *A Mercy*." She ran her thumb over the shell's ridges and then gave it back. She looked at me. "Orphans," she said.

Gramps never spoke about my mother, but he didn't have to. All I had to do was stop by the surf shop or show up at the beach at dawn, and I'd be handed free Mollusk shirts and thermoses full of tea. When I was a kid, my mom's old friends liked to wrap their arms around me, pet my hair. They squinted in my direction as I approached and beckoned me toward them on the sand. I didn't know all of their names, but every one of them knew mine.

I guess when you spend a life riding waves—knowing that the ocean is heartless and millions of times stronger than you are, but still trusting that you're skilled enough or brave enough or charmed enough to survive it—you become indebted to the people who don't make it. Someone always dies. It's just a matter of who, and when. You remember her with songs, with shrines of shells and flowers and beach glass, with an arm around her daughter and, later, daughters of your own named after her.

She didn't actually die in the ocean. She died at Laguna Honda Hospital, a gash on her head, her lungs full of water. I was almost three. Sometimes I think I can remember a warmth. A closeness. A feeling of being in arms, maybe. Soft hair against my cheek.

There is nothing to remember of my father. He was a traveler, back somewhere in Australia before the pregnancy test. "If only he knew about you," Gramps would say when I was little and wondering. "You would be his treasure."

I thought of the grief as simple. Quiet. One photograph of Claire hung in the hallway. Sometimes I caught Gramps looking at it. Sometimes I stood in front of it for several minutes at a time, studying her face and her body. Finding hints of myself in her. Imagining that I must have been nearby, playing in the sand or lying on a blanket. Wondering if, when I was twenty-two, my smile would be anywhere close to that pretty.

Once in a meeting at Convent, the counselor asked Gramps if he talked about my mother with me. "Remembering the departed is the only way to heal," she said.

Gramps's eyes lost their sparkle. His mouth became a tight line.

"Just a reminder," the counselor said more quietly, then turned to the computer screen to get back to the matter of my unexcused absences.

"Sister," Gramps said, his voice low and venomous. "I lost my wife when she was forty-six. I lost my daughter when she was twenty-four. And you *remind* me to remember them?"

"Mr. Delaney," she said. "I am truly sorry for your loss. *Both* of your losses. I will pray for your healing. But my concern here is for Marin, and all I ask is that you share some of your memories with *her*."

My body went tense. We were called in because they were concerned about my "academic progress," but I was getting As or Bs in all my classes and all they had on me was that I'd cut a couple periods. Now I realized that this meeting was actually about a story I'd written, a story in English about a girl raised by sirens. The sirens were guilt-ridden over murdering the girl's mother, so they told the girl stories about her, made her as real as they could, but there was always a hollowness to the girl that they couldn't fill. She was always wondering.

It was only a story, but sitting in the counselor's office I realized I should have known better. I should have written about a prince raised by wolves after he lost his father to the woods or whatever, something less transparent, because teachers always thought everything was a cry for help. And young, nice teachers like Sister Josephine were the worst.

I knew I had to change the subject or the counselor would start talking about my story. "I'm really sorry about the classes I missed, okay?" I said. "It was poor judgment. I got too swept up in my social life."

The counselor nodded.

"May I count on you not to do this again?" she asked. "You have before school and after school. The lunch period. Evenings. Weekends. The majority of your hours are free to spend however you and your grandfather see fit. But during class periods we expect—"

"Sister," Gramps said, his voice a growl again, as if he hadn't heard anything we'd been saying. "I'm sure that painful things have happened to you. Even marrying Jesus can't entirely shield you from the realities of life. I ask you now to take a moment to remember those terrible things. I *remind* you, now, to remember them. There. Don't you feel *healed*? Maybe you should tell us about them. Don't you feel, don't you feel . . . *so much better*? Do they fill you with fondness? Do you find yourself *joyful*?"

"Mr. Delaney, please."

"Would you care to dazzle us with a tale of *redemption*?"

"All right, I can see—"

"Would you like to sing a song of *joy* for us now?"

"I apologize for upsetting you, but this is—"

Gramps stood, puffed out his chest.

"Yes," he said. "This is entirely inappropriate of me. Almost as inappropriate as a nun offering counsel regarding the deaths of a *spouse* and a *child*. Marin is getting excellent grades. Marin is an excellent student." The counselor leaned back in her office chair, stoic. "And Marin," Gramps said, triumphant, "is coming with me!"

He turned and swung open the door.

"Bye," I said, as apologetically as I could.

He stormed out. I followed him.

The car ride home was a one-man comedy act comprised of every nun joke Gramps could remember. I laughed at the punch lines until he didn't really need me anymore. It was a monologue. When it was over I asked him if he'd heard from Birdie today, and he smiled.

"You write two letters, you get two letters," he said.

And then I thought of the tears in Sister Josephine's eyes when I was reading my story to the class. How she thanked me for being so brave. And okay, maybe it wasn't entirely imagined. Maybe the sirens gave the girl shells that filled her underwater room. Maybe the story came from some part of me that wished I knew more, or at least had actual memories instead of feelings that may have only been inventions.

chapter four

MABEL IS LEARNING as much about Hannah as our room can tell her. The pile of papers on her desk, her immaculate bed-making. The signed posters from Broadway shows and her bright, plush comforter.

"Where's she from?"

"Manhattan."

"This is the prettiest blue," Mabel says, admiring the Persian rug between our beds, worn enough to show its age but still soft underfoot.

She stands in front of the bulletin board, asking me about the people in the photographs. Megan, from down the hall. Davis, her ex-boyfriend who is still her friend. Some girls, also from home, whose names I don't remember.

"She likes quotes," Mabel says.

I nod. "She reads a lot."

"This Emerson quote is everywhere. I saw it on a magnet."

"Which one?"

"'Finish each day and be done with it. You have done what you could. Some blunders and absurdities no doubt crept in; forget them as soon as you can.'"

"I can see why. Who doesn't need to be reminded of that?"

"Yeah, I guess so," Mabel says.

"Hannah's really like that," I say. "Things don't seem to get to her. She's kind of . . . straightforward, I guess. But in the best way. In a way that's really smart and kind."

"So you like her."

"Yeah. I like her a lot."

"Great," she says, but I can't tell if she means it. "Okay, let's move on to you. What kind of plant is this?"

"A peperomia. I got it at a plant sale on campus and I've kept it alive for three months. Impressive, right?"

"Good job."

"I know."

We smile at each other. It feels almost natural between us.

"These are nice bowls," she says, taking one off my windowsill.

Besides the photograph of my mother that lives in a folder in my closet, the bowls are the best things I own.

They're a perfect shade of yellow, not too bright, and I know where they came from and who made them. I like how substantial they are, how you can feel the weight of the clay.

"One of the first lectures my history professor gave us was about this guy William Morris. He said that everything you own should be either useful or beautiful. It's a lot to aspire to, but I figured why not try? I saw these in a potter's studio a couple days afterward and I bought them."

"They're so pretty."

"They make everything feel kind of special. Even cereal and ramen," I say. "Which are both major components of my diet."

"Pillars of nutrition."

"What do you eat at school?"

"My dorms are different. Like mini-apartments. We have three rooms and then a common space with a living room and kitchen. Six of us share it so we cook lots of big batches of things. My roommate makes the best lasagna. I have no idea how it's as good as it is—she just uses pre-shredded cheese and bottled sauce."

"At least she has that going for her."

"What do you mean?" she asks.

Before she gave up on me, Mabel sent me a litany of reasons not to like her roommate. Her terrible taste in music, her loud snoring, her tumultuous love life and messiness and ugly decorations. *Remind me why you didn't join me in sunny Southern California?* she wrote. And also: *Please! Come make this girl disappear and steal her identity!*

"Oh," she says now, remembering. "Right. Well, it's been a while. She's grown on me." She turns to see what else she can comment on, but the plant and bowls are the extent of my furnishings.

"I'm planning on getting more stuff soon," I say. "I just need to find a job first."

Concern flashes across her face. "Do you have . . . ? I can't believe I never thought about this. Do you have any money?"

"Yeah," I say. "Don't worry. He left me some, just not that much. I mean, enough for now, but I have to be careful."

"What about tuition?"

"He had already paid for this year."

"But what about the next three years?"

This shouldn't be so difficult to talk about. This part should be easy. "My counselor here says we should be able to make it work. With loans and financial aid and scholarships. She says as long as I do well, we should be able to figure it out."

"Okay," she says. "That sounds good, I guess."

But she still looks concerned.

"So," I say. "You're here for three nights, right?"

She nods.

"I thought maybe tomorrow or the next day we could take the bus to the shopping district. There isn't too much there, but there's the studio where I bought those bowls and a restaurant and a few other shops."

"Yeah, sounds fun."

She's staring at the rug now, not yet back to herself.

"Marin," she says. "I should just tell you now that I'm here with a motive, not for vacation."

My heart sinks, but I try not to let it show. I look at her and wait.

"Come home with me," she says. "My parents want you to come."

"Go for what? Christmas?"

"Yeah, Christmas. But then to stay. I mean, you'd come back here, of course, but you could go back to my house for breaks. It could be your house, too."

"Oh," I say. "When you said *motive*, I thought something else."

"Like what?"

"I don't know."

I can't bring myself to say that I thought it meant she didn't really want to see me, when really she's asking to see me more.

"So will you say yes?"

"I don't think I can."

Her eyebrows rise in surprise. I have to look away from her face.

"I guess that's a lot to ask you all at once. Maybe we should just start with Christmas. Fly back with me, spend a couple days, see how you feel. My parents will pay for your flight."

I shake my head. "I'm sorry."

She's thrown off. This was supposed to go differently. "I have three days to convince you, so just think about it. Pretend you didn't say no. Pretend you haven't answered yet."

I nod, but I know that—no matter how much I want to—it would be impossible for me to go back.

She crosses to Hannah's side of the room and looks at everything again. She unzips her duffel bag and sifts through what she's brought. And then she's back at the window.

"There's another view," I say. "From the top floor. It's really pretty."

We ride the elevator up to the tower. Stepping out with Mabel, I realize it's the kind of place the governess in *The Turn of the Screw* would find rife with ghostly possibilities. I try not to think about stories much anymore, though, especially stories about ghosts.

From the tower windows we can see the rest of the campus, a panoramic view. I thought talking might come easier for us up here, where there's more to see, but I'm still tongue-tied and Mabel is still silent. Angry, probably. I can see it in her shoulders and the way she isn't looking at me.

"Who's that?" she asks.

I follow her pointing hand to someone in the distance. A spot of light.

"The groundskeeper," I say.

We keep watching as he gets closer, stopping every few steps and crouching down.

"He's doing something along the path," Mabel says.

"Yeah. I wonder what."

When he reaches the front of our building, he steps back and looks up. He's waving at us. We wave back.

"Do you know each other?"

"No," I say. "But he knows I'm here. I guess he's kind of in charge of keeping track of me. Or at least of making sure I don't burn the school down or throw a wild party or something."

"Both highly likely."

I can't muster a smile. Even with the knowledge that it's dark outside and light up here, it's hard to believe that he can see us. We should be invisible. We are so alone. Mabel and I are standing side by side, but we can't even see each other. In the distance are the lights of town. People must be finishing their workdays, picking up their kids, figuring out dinner. They're talking to one another in easy voices about things of great significance and things that don't mean much. The distance between us and all of that living feels insurmountable.

The groundskeeper climbs into his truck.

I say, "I was afraid to ride the elevator."

"What do you mean?"

"It was before you got here. On my way to the store. I was about to ride the elevator down but then I was afraid that I'd get stuck and no one would know. You would have gotten here and I wouldn't have had any reception."

"Do the elevators here get stuck?"

"I don't know."

"Have you *heard* of them getting stuck?"

"No. But they're old."

She walks away from me, toward the elevator. I follow her.

"It's so fancy," she says.

Like so much of this building, every detail is ornate. Etched brass with leaf motifs and plaster swirls above the door. Places aren't this old in California. I'm used to simple lines. I'm used to being closer to the ground. Mabel presses the button and the doors open like they've been waiting for us. I pull the metal gates apart and we step inside where the walls are wood paneled, lit by a chandelier. The doors close and we're in the space for the third time today but, for the first time, we are in the moment together.

Until, mid-descent, when Mabel reaches toward the

control panel and presses a button that makes us jolt to a stop.

"What are you doing?"

"Let's just see how it feels," she says. "It might be good for you."

I shake my head. This isn't funny. The groundskeeper saw that we were fine. He drove away. We could be stuck here for days before he'd begin to worry. I search the control panel for a button that will get us moving again, but Mabel says, "It's right here. We can press it whenever we want to."

"I want to press it now."

"Really?"

She isn't taunting me. It's a real question. Do I really want us to move again so soon. Do I really want to be back on the third floor with her, nowhere to go but back to my room, nothing waiting there for us that wasn't there before, no newfound ease or understanding.

"Okay," I say. "Maybe not."

"I've been thinking about your grandpa a lot," Mabel says.

We've been sitting on the elevator floor, each leaning against a separate wall, for a few minutes now. We've discussed the details of the buttons, the refracted light from the crystals on the chandelier. We've searched our vocabularies for the name of the wood and settled on mahogany. And now, I guess, Mabel thinks it's time to move on to topics of greater importance.

"God, he was cute."

"Cute? No."

"Okay, I'm sorry. That sounds patronizing. I just mean those glasses! Those sweaters with the elbow patches! *Real* ones that he sewed on himself because the sleeves wore through. He was the real deal."

"I know what you're saying," I tell her. "And I'm telling you that it isn't right."

The edge in my voice is impossible to miss, but I'm not sorry. Every time I think about him, a black pit blooms in my stomach and breathing becomes a struggle.

"Okay." Her voice has become quieter. "I'm doing this wrong. That's not even what I meant to say. I was trying to say that I loved him. I miss him. I know it's only a fraction of how you must feel, but I miss him and I thought you might want to know that someone else is thinking about him."

I nod. I don't know what else to do. I want to get him out of my head.

"I wish there had been a memorial," she says. "My parents and I kept expecting to hear about it. I was just waiting for the dates to book my ticket." And now the edge is in her voice, because I didn't respond the way I should have, I guess, and because he and I were each other's only family. Mabel's parents offered to help me plan a service, but

I didn't call them back. Sister Josephine called, too, but I ignored her. Jones left me voice mails that I never picked up. Because instead of grieving like a normal person, I ran away to New York even though the dorms wouldn't be open for another two weeks. I stayed in a motel and kept the television on all day. I ate all my meals in the same twenty-four-hour diner and I kept no semblance of a schedule. Every time my phone rang the sound rattled my bones. But when I turned it off I was entirely alone, and I kept waiting for him to call, to tell me everything was fine.

And I was afraid of his ghost.

And I was sick with myself.

I slept with my head under blankets and each time I stepped outside in the daylight I thought I'd go blind.

"Marin," Mabel says. "I came all the way here so that when I talked, you'd be forced to talk back."

The television played soap operas. Commercials for car dealerships, paper towels, dish soap. *Judge Judy* and *Geraldo*. Always, Dove, Swiffer. Laugh tracks. Close-ups of tear-stained faces. Shirts unbuttoning, laughter. Objection, your honor. Sustained.

"I started to think you must have lost your phone. Or that you hadn't taken it with you. I felt like a stalker. All of those calls and emails and text messages. Do you have any idea how many times I tried to reach you?" Her eyes tear up. A bitter laugh escapes her. "What a stupid question," she says. "Of course you do. Because you got them all and just decided not to respond."

"*I didn't know what to say,*" I whisper. It sounds so inadequate, even to me.

"Maybe you could tell me how you came to that decision. I've been wondering what exactly I did to bring about that specific strategy."

"It wasn't strategic."

"Then what was it? I've spent all this time telling myself that what you're going through is so much bigger than you not talking to me. Sometimes it works. But sometimes it doesn't."

"What happened with him . . . ," I say. "What happened at the end of the summer . . . It was more than you know."

Amazing, how difficult these words are. They are barely anything. I know that. But they terrify me. Because even with the healing I've done, and the many ways in which I've pulled myself together, I haven't said any of this out loud.

"Well," she says. "I'm listening."

"I had to leave."

"You just *disappeared.*"

"No. I didn't. I came *here.*"

The words make sense, but deeper than the words is the truth. She's right. If Mabel's talking about the girl who hugged her good-bye before she left for Los Angeles, who laced fingers with her at the last bonfire of the summer and accepted shells from almost-strangers, who analyzed novels for fun and lived with her grandfather in a pink, rent-controlled house in the Sunset that often smelled like cake and was often filled with elderly, gambling men—if she's talking about that girl, then yes, I disappeared.

But it's so much simpler not to look at it that way, so I add, "I've been here the whole time."

"I had to fly three thousand miles to find you."

"I'm glad you did."

"Are you?"

"Yes."

She looks at me, trying to see if I mean it.

"*Yes*," I say again.

She pushes her hair behind her ear. I watch her. I've been trying not to look too closely. She was kind enough to pretend she didn't notice me holding on to her scarf and hat earlier; I don't need to test my luck. But again, it hits me: *Here she is*. Her fingers, her long, dark hair. Her pink lips and black eyelashes. The same gold earrings she never takes out, not even when she sleeps.

"Okay," she says.

She presses a button and here is movement after so many minutes of suspension.

Down, down. I'm not sure I'm ready. But now we're on

the third floor, and Mabel and I reach for the gate at the same time, and our hands touch.

She pulls back before I know what I want.

"Sorry," she says. She isn't apologizing for pulling away. She's apologizing for our accidental contact.

We used to touch all the time, even before we really knew each other. Our first conversation began with her grabbing my hand to examine my newly painted nails, gold with silver moons. Jones's daughter, Samantha, ran a salon and she had her new hires practice on me. I told Mabel I could probably get her a discount on a manicure there.

She said, "Maybe *you* could just do it? It can't be that hard." So after school we went to Walgreens for nail polish and we sat in Lafayette Park while I made a mess of her fingertips and we laughed for hours.

Mabel's ahead of me, almost to my doorway.

Wait.

Not enough has changed yet.

"Do you remember the first day we hung out?" I ask.

She stops walking. Turns to me.

"At the park?"

"Yes," I say. "Yes. And I tried to paint your nails because you liked mine, and they turned out terribly."

She shrugs. "I don't remember it being that bad."

"No. *It* wasn't bad. Just my nail-painting skills."

"I thought we had fun."

"Of course we had fun. It's what made us become friends. You thought I'd be able to give you a manicure and I failed miserably, but we laughed a lot, and that's how it all started."

Mabel leans against the doorway. She stares down the hall.

"How it all started was in the first day of English, when Brother John had us analyze some stupid poem, and you raised your hand and said something so smart about it that suddenly the poem didn't seem stupid anymore. And I knew that you were the kind of person I wanted to know. But what I *didn't* know yet was that you can tell a girl you want to hang out with her because she said something smart. So I looked for an excuse to talk to you, and I found one."

She's never told me this before.

"It wasn't about a *manicure*," she says. She shakes her head as though the idea were absurd, even though it's the only version of the story I've known until now. Then she turns and goes into my room.

"What have you been doing for dinner?" she asks.

I gesture toward the desk, where an electric kettle rests next to packages of Top Ramen.

"Well, let's do it."

"I bought food," I say. "There's a kitchen we can use."

She shakes her head.

"It's been a long day. Ramen is fine."

She sounds so tired. Tired of me and the way I'm not talking.

I take my usual trip to the bathroom sink for water, and then plug in the electric kettle at my desk and set the yellow bowls next to it. Here comes another chance. I try to think of something to say.

But Mabel rushes in before me.

"There's something I need to tell you."

"Okay."

"I met someone at school. His name is Jacob."

I can't help the surprise on my face.

"When?"

"About a month ago. You know the nine hundredth text and phone call you decided to ignore?"

I turn away from her. Pretend to check something on the kettle.

"He's in my literature class. I really like him," she says, voice gentler now.

I watch until the first puffs of steam escape, and then I ask, "Does he know about me?"

She doesn't answer. I pour water into the bowls, over the dried noodles. Tear open the flavor packets. Sprinkle the powder over the surface. Stir. And then there is nothing to do but wait, so I'm forced to turn back.

"He knows that I have a best friend named Marin, who was raised by a grandfather I loved like my own. He knows that I left for school and a few days later Gramps drowned, and that ever since the night it happened my friend Marin hasn't spoken to anyone back home. Not even to me."

I wipe tears off my face with the back of one hand.

I wait.

"And he knows that things between us got . . . less clearly defined toward the end. And he's fine with that."

I search my memory for the way we used to talk about boys. What is it that I might have said back then? I would have asked to see a picture. I'm sure there are dozens on her phone.

But I don't want to see his picture.

I have to say something.

"He sounds nice," I blurt. And then I realize that she's barely told me anything about him. "I mean, I'm sure you would choose someone nice."

I feel her staring, but that's all I have in me.

We eat in silence.

"There's a rec room on the fourth floor," I say when we're finished. "We could watch a movie if you want."

"I'm actually pretty tired," she says. "I think I might just get ready for bed."

"Oh, sure." I glance at the clock. It's just a few minutes past nine, and three hours earlier in California.

"Your roommate won't mind?" she asks, pointing to Hannah's bed.

"No, it's fine." I can barely get the words out.

"Okay, great. I'm going to get ready, then."

She gathers her toiletries bag and her pajamas, picks up her phone quickly, as though I might not notice, and slips out of the room.

She's away for a long time. Ten minutes pass, then another ten, then another. I wish I could do something besides sit and wait for her.

I hear her laugh. I hear her grow serious.

She says, "You have nothing to worry about."

She says, "I promise."

She says, "I love you, too."

chapter five

I COPIED DOWN all the passages about ghosts I could find and spread them over the coffee table, sorted them, and read them each dozens of times. I was beginning to think that it was never the ghosts themselves that were important. Like Mabel had said, all they did was stand around.

It wasn't the ghosts. It was the hauntings that mattered.

The ghosts told the governess that she would never know love.

The ghost told Jane Eyre that she was alone.

The ghost told the Buendía family that their worst fears were right: They were doomed to repeat the same mistakes.

I scribbled some notes and then I took *Jane Eyre* and stretched out on the couch. Along with my other favorite novel, *One Hundred Years of Solitude*, I'd read it more times than I could count. While *One Hundred Years of Solitude* swept me up in its magic and its images, its intricacies and its breadth, *Jane Eyre* made my heart swell. Jane was so lonely. She was so strong and sincere and honest. I loved them both, but they satisfied different longings.

Just as Rochester was about to propose, I heard Gramps downstairs jangling his keys, and a moment later he walked in whistling.

"Good mail day?" I asked him.

"You write a letter, you get a letter."

"You two are so reliable."

I ran downstairs to help him carry up the grocery bags and put the food away, and then I went back to *Jane Eyre* and he disappeared into his study. I liked to imagine him reading the letters in there by himself, in his recliner with his cigarettes and crystal ashtray. The window open to the salty air and his lips mouthing the words.

I used to wonder what kinds of letters he wrote. I'd caught glimpses of old poetry books stacked on his desk. I wondered if he quoted them. Or if he wrote his own verses, or stole lines and passed them off as his own.

And who was this Birdie? She must have been the sweetest of ladies. Waiting for Gramps's letters. Composing her own to him. I pictured her in a chair on a veranda, sipping iced teas and writing with perfect penmanship. When she wasn't writing to my grandfather, she was probably training bougainvillea vines or painting water-color landscapes.

Or maybe she was wilder than that. Maybe she was the kind of grandma who cursed and went out dancing, who had a devious spark in her eyes that would rival Gramps's. Maybe she would beat him at poker, smoke cigarettes with him late into the night once they found a way to be together instead of several states apart. Once I wasn't holding him back anymore.

Sometimes the thought of that kept me up at night, gave me a sick feeling in my stomach. If it weren't for me, maybe he'd leave San Francisco for the Rocky Mountains. Besides me, all he had here were Jones and Freeman and Bo, and he didn't even seem to like them much anymore. They still played cards like they always did, but there was less laughter among them.

"May I interrupt your reading? I got something very special today," Gramps said.

He was back in the living room, smiling at me.

"Show me."

"Okay," he said. "But I'm afraid you won't be able to touch it. It's fragile."

"I'll be careful."

"You just sit here, and I'll hold it up and show you."

I rolled my eyes.

"Now, Sailor," he said. "Don't do that. Don't be like that. This is something special."

He looked pained, and I was sorry.

"I'll only look," I said.

He nodded.

"I'm excited," I said.

"I'll get it. Wait here."

He came out with fabric folded in his hands, a deep green, and he let it unfurl and I saw it was a dress.

I cocked my head.

"Birdie's," he said.

"She sent you her dress?"

"I wanted to have something from her. I told her to surprise me. Does it count as a gift if you ask for it?"

I shrugged. "Sure."

Something struck me about the dress. The straps were scalloped; white and pink embroidery decorated the waist.

"It looks like something a young woman would wear."

Gramps smiled.

"Such a sharp girl," he said approvingly. "This dress is from when she was young. She said she didn't mind sending it, because she isn't as slight as she used to be. It doesn't fit her and it's not appropriate for a lady of her age."

He took another long look at the dress, and then he folded the sides in and rolled it down from the top so that it never left his hands. He hugged it to his chest.

"It's beautiful," I said.

Later, while he washed the dinner dishes and I dried, I asked, "Gramps, why don't you ever talk about Birdie with the guys?"

He grinned at me. "Wouldn't want to rub it in," he said. "Not everyone can have what Birdie and I have."

A few days later, I was on the floor in Mabel's living room, looking through photo albums. "I was *not* the most beautiful newborn," Mabel said.

"What are you *talking* about? You were perfect. A perfect little grasshopper. How about that one!" Ana pointed to a photograph of Mabel wrapped in a white blanket, yawning.

"I want something more . . . alert."

All the seniors had been tasked with submitting a baby photo for the yearbook, and the deadline was soon. Eleanor, that year's editor, grew closer to a nervous breakdown with each day that passed. Her voice over the intercom during the daily announcements had become shrill. "*Please*," she'd say. "Please just email me something *soon*."

"Have you chosen yours yet?" Ana asked, returning to the sofa to get back to the drawing she was doing.

"We don't have any."

She turned to a new page in her sketchbook.

"None?"

"I don't think so. He's never shown me anything."

"May I draw you?"

"Really?"

"Just a ten-minute sketch."

She patted the sofa cushion next to her and I sat. She studied my face before she touched charcoal to paper. She looked at my eyes, my ears, the slant of my nose, my cheekbones and my neck and the tiny freckles across my cheeks that no one ever noticed. She reached out and untucked my hair from behind one of my ears so that it fell forward.

She began to draw, and I looked at her as if I were drawing her, too. Her eyes and her ears and the slant of *her* nose. The flush in her cheeks and her laugh lines. The flecks of lighter brown in the darker brown of her eyes. She'd turn to her page and then look up at some part of me. I found myself waiting, each time she glanced down, for her to look at me again.

"Okay, I found two," Mabel said. "This one says I'm ten months and I finally look like a human. This one is less baby, more toddler, but it's pretty cute, if I do say so myself."

She dangled them in front of us.

"Can't lose," Ana said, beaming at the sight of them.

"I vote baby," I said. "Those chubby thighs! Adorable."

She went off to scan and send it, and Ana and I were alone in the living room.

"Just a few more minutes," she told me.

"Okay."

"Want to see?" she asked when she was done.

I nodded, and she laid the book in my lap. The girl on the page was me and she wasn't. I'd never seen a drawing of myself before.

"Look." Ana showed me her hands, covered in charcoal. "I need to wash up, but I'm thinking about something. Follow me?" I followed her across the room to the kitchen where she turned the brass faucet handle with her wrist and let the water run over her hands. "I think he must have something to share with you. Even if he doesn't have *many* photos, he's bound to have at least one or two."

"What if he didn't end up with my mom's stuff?"

"You're his granddaughter. You were almost three when she died, yes? He would have had a photograph of his own by then." She dried her hands on a bright green dish towel. "Ask him. I think, if you ask him, he will find *something*."

When I got home, Gramps was drinking tea in the kitchen. I knew it was then or never. I would lose the courage if I waited until morning.

"So we're supposed to turn in baby pictures for yearbook. For the senior pages. I'm wondering, do you think you have one somewhere?" I shifted my weight from one foot to the other. I heard my voice go high-pitched and shaky. "Or, like, it doesn't have to be *baby* baby. I could be two or three in it. Just little. I think we don't have any, which is fine, but I'm supposed to ask."

Gramps was very still. He stared into his teacup.

"I'll look through some storage. See if I can find something."

"That would be great."

He opened his mouth to say something, but must have changed his mind. The next day after school when I came inside, he was waiting for me in the living room. He didn't look at me.

"Sailor," he said. "I tried but—"

"It's okay," I rushed in.

"So much was lost."

"I know." I was sorry I was making him say this, sorry to have brought back memories of what was lost. I thought of the way he yelled at my counselor. "You *remind* me to remember them?"

"Really, Gramps." He still couldn't look at me. "*Really*. It's fine."

I'd known better, but had asked anyway. I was sick with the way I'd upset him and sick, also, with the way I'd let myself hope for something that didn't exist.

I walked along Ocean Beach for a long time, until I reached the rocks below the Cliff House, and then I turned around. When I was back where I started, I still wasn't ready to go home, so I sat on a dune and watched the waves in the afternoon sun. A woman with long brown hair and a wet suit was nearby, and after a while she came to sit next to me.

"Hey," she said. "I'm Emily. I was one of Claire's friends."

"Yeah, I recognize you."

"He's been coming here more often, right?" She pointed to the water's edge, and there was Gramps in the distance, walking alone. "I hadn't seen him for a long time. Now I see him almost every week."

I couldn't answer her. Besides his trips to the grocery store and his clockwork poker games, Gramps's comings and goings were mysteries to me. I'd run into him on the beach a few times, but I wasn't usually here at this time in the afternoon.

"He was a good surfer," she said. "Better than a lot of us, even though he was older."

Gramps never talked to me about surfing, but sometimes he'd make comments about the waves that showed he knew a lot about the water. I had suspected that he'd been a surfer at some point in his life, but I hadn't ever asked him.

"There was this day," Emily said. "A couple months after Claire died. Do you know this story?"

"I might?" I said, even though I didn't know any stories. "Tell it to me anyway."

"None of us had seen him out there since we'd lost her.

It was a Saturday, and so many of us were out. He appeared with his board on the sand. Some of us saw him, and we knew that we had to do something. To show our respect, let him see our grief. So we got out of the water. We called out to the others, who hadn't seen him. It didn't take long until there was only him in the water, and all of us were lined up on the sand in our suits, watching. We stayed like that for a long time. I don't remember how long, but we stayed like that until he was done. When he finished, he paddled back, tucked his board under his arm, and walked right past us, like we were invisible. I don't even know if he noticed us there."

He was closer to us now, but I knew that he wouldn't look around and see me and I decided against calling to him. A wave crashed in, took him by surprise, but he barely tried to dodge it. It soaked his pants legs up to the knees, but he kept walking as though nothing had happened.

Emily's brow furrowed.

"I know I don't need to tell you this," she said. "But it can be dangerous out here. Even just walking."

"Yeah," I said, and I felt fear rush in, compounding my guilt. Did I dredge up memories he'd worked hard to forget? Did I drive him out here with my request? "I should say something to him about it."

She kept watching him. "He already knows."

chapter six

WE'RE WAITING AT THE BUS STOP in the snow.

Mabel was already showered and dressed by the time I woke up. I opened my eyes and she said, "Let's go somewhere for breakfast. I want to see more of this town." But I knew that what she really wanted was to be somewhere else, where it wasn't the two of us trapped in a room thick with the things we weren't saying.

So now we're on the side of a street covered in white, trees and mountains in every direction. Once in a while a car passes us and its color stands out against the snow.

A blue car.

A red car.

"My toes are numb," Mabel says.

"Mine, too."

A black car, a green one.

"I can't feel my face."

"Me, neither."

Mabel and I have boarded buses together thousands of times, but when the bus appears in the distance it's entirely unfamiliar. It's the wrong landscape, the wrong color, the wrong bus name and number, the wrong fare, and the wrong accent when the driver says, "You heard about the storm, right?"

We take halting, interrupted steps, not knowing how far back we should go or who should duck into a row first. She steps to the side to make me lead, as though just because I live here I know which seat would be right for us. I keep walking until we're out of choices. We sit in the center of the back.

I don't know what a storm here would mean. The snow is so soft when it falls, nothing like hail. Not even like rain so hard it wakes you up or the kind of wind that hurls tree branches into the streets.

The bus inches along even though there's no traffic.

"Dunkin' Donuts," Mabel says. "I've heard of that."

"Everyone likes their coffee."

"Is it good?"

I shrug. "It's not like the coffee we're used to."

"Because it's just coffee-coffee?"

I pull at a loose stitch in the fingertip of my glove.

"I actually haven't tried it."

"Oh."

"I think it's like diner coffee," I say.

I stay away from diners now. Whenever Hannah or her friends suggest going out to eat, I make sure to get the name of the place first and look it up. They tease me for being a food snob, an easy misunderstanding to play along with, but I'm not that picky about what I eat. I'm just afraid that one day something's going to catch me by surprise. Stale coffee. Squares of American cheese. Hard tomatoes, so unripe they're white in the center. The most innocent things can call back the most terrible.

I want to be closer to a window, so I scoot down the row. The glass is freezing, even through my glove, and now that we're closer to the shopping district, lights line the street, strung from streetlamp to streetlamp.

All my life, winter has meant gray skies and rain, puddles and umbrellas. Winter has never looked like this.

Wreathes on every door. Menorahs on windowsills. Christmas trees sparkling through parted curtains. I press my forehead to the glass, catch my reflection. I want to be part of the world outside.

We reach our stop and step into the cold, and the bus pulls away to reveal a lit-up tree with gold ornaments in the middle of the square.

My heart swells.

As anti-religion as Gramps was, he was all about the spectacle. Each year we bought a tree from Delancey Street. Guys with prison tattoos tied the tree to the roof of the car, and we heaved it up the stairs ourselves. I'd get the decorations down from the hall closet. They were all old. I didn't know which ones had been my mother's and which were older than that, but it didn't matter. They were my only evidence of a family larger than him and me. We might have been all that was left, but we were still a part of something bigger. Gramps would bake cookies and make eggnog from scratch. We'd listen to Christmas music on the radio and hang ornaments, then sit on the sofa and lean back with our mugs and crumb-covered plates to admire our work.

"Jesus Christ," he'd say. "Now, that's a *tree*."

The memory has barely surfaced, but already it's begun. The doubt creeps in. *Is that how it really was?* The sickness settles in my stomach. *You thought you knew him.*

I want to buy gifts for people.

Something for Mabel. Something to send back for Ana and Javier. Something to leave on Hannah's bed for when she returns from break or to take with me to Manhattan if I really go to see her.

The window of the potter's studio is lit. It seems too early for it to be open, but I squint and see that the sign in the window says COME IN.

The first time I came here was in the fall, and I was too nervous to look closely at everything. It was my first time out with Hannah and her friends. I kept telling myself to act normal, to laugh along with everyone else, to say something once in a while. They didn't want to spend too long inside— we were wandering in and out of shops—but everything was beautiful and I couldn't imagine leaving empty-handed.

I chose the yellow bowls. They were heavy and cheerful, the perfect size for cereal or soup. Now every time Hannah uses one she sighs and says she wishes she'd bought some for herself.

No one is behind the counter when Mabel and I walk in, but the store is warm and bright, full of earth tones and tinted glazes. A wood-burning stove glows with heat, and a scarf is slung over a wooden chair.

I head toward the shelves of bowls first for Hannah's gift. I thought I'd buy her a pair that matched mine, but there are more colors now, including a mossy green that I know she'd love. I take two of them and glance at Mabel. I want her to like this place.

She's found a row of large bells that dangle from thick rope. Each bell is a different color and size, each has a pattern carved into it. She rings one and smiles at the sound it makes. I feel like I've done something right in taking her here.

"Oh, hi!" A woman appears from a doorway behind the counter, holding up her clay-covered hands. I remember her from the first time. For some reason it hadn't occurred to me then that she was the potter, but knowing it makes everything even better.

"I've seen you before," she says.

"I came in a couple months ago with my roommate."

"Welcome back," she says. "It's nice to see you again."

"I'm going to set these on the counter while I keep looking," I say, holding out the green bowls.

"Yes, sure. Let me know if you need me. I'll just be back here finishing something up."

I set the bowls next to a stack of postcards inviting people to a three-year-anniversary party. I would have thought the store had been here longer. It's so warm and lived-in. I wonder what she did before she was here. She's probably Mabel's parents' age, with gray-blond hair swept back in a barrette and lines by her eyes when she smiles. I didn't notice if she wore a wedding ring. I don't know why, but I feel like something happened to her, like there's pain behind her smile. I felt it the first time. When she took my money, I felt like she wanted to keep me here. I wonder if there's a secret current that connects people who have lost something. Not in the way that everyone loses something, but in the way that undoes your life, undoes your self, so that when you look at your face it isn't yours anymore.

"Who are the bowls for?" Mabel asks.

"Hannah."

She nods.

"I want to get your parents a present, too," I say. "Do you think they'd like something from here?"

"Anything," she says. "Everything here is so nice."

We look at some things together and then I make another round and Mabel drifts back to the bells. I see her check the price of one of them. Ana and Javier keep flowers in every room of their house, so I take a closer look at a corner of vases.

"How's this?" I ask her, holding up a round one. It's a dusty-pink color, subtle enough that it would work in their brightest rooms.

"Perfect," she says. "They'll love it."

I choose a gift for myself, too: a pot for my peperomia, in the same color as Ana and Javier's vase. I've kept my little plant in its plastic pot for too long, and this will look so much prettier.

The potter is sitting at the counter now, making notes on a piece of paper, and when I take the vase up to her I'm seized with the wish to stay. I hand her my ATM card when she gives me the total, and then I work up the courage to ask.

"I was wondering," I say as she wraps the first bowl up in tissue paper. "By any chance, are you hiring?"

"Oh," she says. "I wish! But it's just me. It's a tiny operation."

"Okay," I say, trying not to sound too disappointed. "I just really love your shop so I thought I'd ask."

She pauses her wrapping. "Thank you." She smiles at me. Soon she's handing me the bag with the wrapped-up vase and dishes, and Mabel and I head back onto the snowy street.

We hurry past a pet store and a post office and into the café, both of us shivering. Only one table is occupied and the waitress looks surprised to see us. She takes a couple menus from a stack.

"We're closing up early because of the storm," she says. "But we can get you fed before then if you can make it quick."

"Sure," I say.

"Yeah," Mabel says. "That's fine."

"Can I get you started with some coffee or orange juice?"

"Cappuccino?" I ask.

She nods.

"Same for me," Mabel says. "And I'll just have a short stack of pancakes."

I scan the menu. "Eggs Benedict, please."

"Thank you, ladies," she says. "And just, excuse my reach for a second . . ."

She leans over our table and turns the sign in the window so that it says CLOSED on the outside. But on our side, perfectly positioned between Mabel's place and mine, it says OPEN. If this were a short story, it would mean something.

The waitress leaves and we turn back to the window. The snow is falling differently; there's more of it in the sky.

"I can't believe you live in a place this cold."

"I know."

We watch in silence. Soon, our coffees arrive.

"It's so pretty, though," I say. "Isn't it?"

"Yeah. It is."

She reaches for the dish of sugar packets, takes out a pink one, a white one, a blue. She lines them up, then reaches for more. I don't know what to make of her nervous hands and faraway expression. Her mouth is a tight line. At another point in my life, I would have leaned across the table and kissed her. At a point further back, I would have sabotaged her, scattered the packets across the table. If I were to go all the way to when we first knew each other, I would have built a careful pattern of my own and both of ours would have expanded until they met in the middle.

"Can we return to the reason I came here?" Mabel asks.

My body tenses. I wonder if she can see it.

I don't want her to list all the reasons I should go back to San Francisco, back to her parents' house, because

I know that they'll all be right. I won't be able to fight against them with any kind of logic. I'll only look foolish or ungrateful.

"I want to say yes," I tell her.

"But you can. You just have to let yourself. You used to spend half your time over there anyway."

She's right.

"We'll be able to see each other on all our breaks, and you'll have a place you can always go home to. My parents want to help you with things when you need it. Like money or just advice or whatever. We can be like sisters," she says. And then she freezes.

A drop of my heart, a ringing in my head.

I smooth my hair behind my ear. I look at the snow.

"I didn't . . ." She leans forward, cradles her head in her hands.

And I think of how time passes so differently for different people. Mabel and Jacob, their months in Los Angeles, months full of doing and seeing and going. Road trips, the ocean. So much living crammed into every day. And then me in my room. Watering my plant. Making ramen. Cleaning my yellow bowls night after night after night.

"It's okay," I say. But it isn't.

Too much time passes and she still hasn't moved.

"I know what you meant," I say.

Our plates of food appear on the table. A bottle of maple

syrup. Ketchup for my home fries. We busy ourselves with eating, but neither of us seems hungry. Right as the check comes, Mabel's phone rings. She drops her credit card onto the bill.

"I got this, okay?" she says. "I'll be right back."

She takes her phone to the back of the restaurant and slides into an empty booth, her back to me.

I abandon our table.

The snow is falling harder now. The pet store clerk hangs a CLOSED sign in its window, but I'm relieved to find the pottery studio's door opens when I push it.

"Again!" she says.

I smile. I'm a little embarrassed to be back, but I can tell she's pleased when I set the bell on the counter.

"I didn't want my friend to see it," I explain.

"I could wrap it in tissue and you could stick it in your coat?" she says.

"Perfect."

She moves quickly, knowing I'm in a hurry, but then pauses.

"How many hours a week would you be looking for?" she asks. "For the job."

"I'm open to pretty much anything."

"After you left I was thinking . . . I really *could* use a hand. But I could only pay minimum wage, and only a couple shifts per week."

"That would be great," I say. "I have classes, so I need time to study. A couple shifts would be great."

"Are you interested in making pottery? Maybe we could work something out where you get to use the kiln. To make up for the fact I can't pay very much."

A warmth passes through me.

"Really?"

She smiles.

"Yes," she says. "I'm Claudia."

"I'm Marin."

"*Marin.* Are you from California?"

I nod.

"I spent a few months in Fairfax. I walked in the redwoods every day."

I force a smile. She's waiting for me to say more, but I don't know what to tell her.

"You must be in the middle of your school break . . . but you're still here."

Worry darts behind her eyes. I wonder what she sees behind mine. *Please don't fuck this up*, I tell myself.

"Fairfax is beautiful," I tell her. "I'm actually from San Francisco, but my family doesn't live there anymore. Can I give you my contact info? And then you can let me know if you do end up wanting help?"

"Yes," Claudia says, handing me a notepad and a pen.

When I give it back to her, she says, "You'll hear from me in early January. Right after the New Year."

"I can't wait."

"Bye, Marin." She holds out the bell, wrapped in tissue. Before she lets go, she locks eyes with me and says, "Have a beautiful holiday."

"You, too." My eyes sting as I walk outside.

Back in the café, Mabel isn't in the booth but she's not at our table either, so I slip her bell inside the bag with the other gifts and wait. I imagine myself in the pottery studio. I'm taking money from a customer and counting change. I'm wrapping yellow bowls in tissue paper and saying, *I have these, too.* I'm saying, *Welcome.* I'm saying, *Happy New Year.* I'm dusting shelves and mopping the tiled floor. Learning to build a fire in the stove.

"Sorry," Mabel says, sliding in across from me.

The waitress appears a moment later.

"You're back! I thought you two left in a panic and forgot your credit card."

"Where were *you?*" Mabel asks me.

I shrug. "I guess I disappeared for a minute."

"Well," she says. "You've gotten good at that."

chapter seven

ANA WAS OUTSIDE when we opened the gate to Mabel's front garden. She was dressed in her painting smock, her hair pinned messily in gold barrettes, staring at her latest collage with a paintbrush and a piece of yarn in her hand.

"Girls!" she said. "I need you."

I'd caught glimpses of her works in progress for the three and a half years I'd been friends with Mabel. Each time I'd felt a rush, and now there was a new reverence to the moment. Ana's collages had been shown by famous galleries in San Francisco and New York and Mexico City for years, but in the last few months she'd sold work to three different museums. Her photograph had begun appearing in magazines. Javier would open them to the articles on Ana and then leave them in prominent places throughout the

house. Ana threw up her hands each time she saw one before snatching it up and stuffing it away. "I'll get a big head,"
she told us. "Hide that away from me."

"It's more simple than usual," Mabel said now, and at
first that seemed true.

It was a night sky, smooth layers of black on black, with
stars shining so bright they almost glittered. I stepped closer.
The stars *did* glitter.

"How did you do that?" I asked.

Ana pointed to a bowl of shining rocks.

"It's fool's gold," she said. "I turned it into a powder."

There was so much going on under the top layer. It was
quiet, maybe, but it wasn't simple.

"I can't decide what to add. It needs something, but I
don't know what. I've tried these feathers. I've tried rope. I
want something nautical. I *think.*"

I understood how she'd feel stuck. What she had was so
beautiful. How could she add something to it without taking
something away?

"Anyway," she said, setting down her paintbrushes.
"How are my girls this evening? Been shopping, I see."

We'd spent an hour in Forever 21 trying on dresses for
Ben's party and now we had matching bags, each contain-
ing a dress identical but for the color. Mabel's was red and
mine was black.

"Have you eaten? Javier made pozole."

"The party already started so we have to be quick . . . ," Mabel said.

"Take it up to your room."

"I can't wait to see what you decide to do."

Ana turned back to her canvas and sighed.

"Me, too, Marin. Me, too."

We started with our makeup, applying eye shadow between bites of soup and tostadas. Mabel emptied her jewelry box onto her bed, and we combed through it for accessories. I chose gold bangles and sparkly green earrings. Mabel chose a braided leather bracelet. She thought about switching her gold studs for another pair, but decided to keep them in. We crunched tostadas, finished all the soup in our bowls. We pulled off our shirts and slipped on the dresses, stepped out of our jeans and looked at each other.

"Just different enough," I said.

"As usual."

Since we'd met, we had a thing for our names' symmetry. An *M* followed by a vowel, then a consonant, then a vowel, then a consonant. We thought it was important. We thought it must have meant something. Like a similar feeling must have passed through our mothers as they named us. Like destiny was at work already. We may have been in different countries, but it was only a matter of time before we would collide into each other.

We were getting ready for the party, but the time was getting later and we weren't hurrying. The real event was us, in her room. We kept reassessing our makeup even though we barely wore any. We showed each other our empty soup bowls and went back into the kitchen for more.

We were on our way back up to Mabel's room when I heard Ana and Javier talking in their living room.

"Such good soup!" I called to Javier, and Ana called back, "Let us see our beautiful girls!"

They were sprawled on a sofa together, Javier with a book, Ana sifting through a box of scraps and small objects, her mind still on her collage, trying to solve the mystery of what should come next.

"Oh!" Ana said when she saw us, dismay on her face.

"*No, no-no-no-no,*" Javier said.

"What's that supposed to mean?" Mabel asked.

"It means you aren't leaving the house in that dress," Javier said.

"You guys," Mabel said. "Seriously?"

Javier said something stern in Spanish, and Mabel's face flushed with indignation.

"*Mom,*" she said.

Ana looked back and forth between Mabel and me. Her gaze landed on Mabel and she said, "It looks like lingerie. I'm sorry, *mi amor*, but you can't go out like this."

"*Mom,*" Mabel said. "Now we don't have any time!"

"You have plenty of clothes," Javier said.

"What about that yellow dress?" Ana asked.

Mabel sighed and stormed up the stairs, and I found myself still standing before them, wearing the same dress as their daughter and waiting for them to tell me something. I felt the heat rise in my face, too, but from embarrassment, not indignation. I wanted to know what it felt like. I wanted them to tell me no.

Javier was already back to his book, but Ana was looking at me. I could tell she was deciding something. I still don't know what she would have said if I had waited a little bit longer. If she would have said anything. But the possibility that she might not tell me to change was crushing. Gramps never looked at my clothes.

I didn't wait around to see if her eyes would find their way back and if the right words would follow. I heard Mabel's door slam and I ran up after her. She was digging through her drawers and saying how stupid all her clothes were, even the good things, but I didn't listen because I was trying to figure out what to do. I had the pair of jeans that I'd worn over but my shirt was too plain. So I took off the dress and picked up the scissors Mabel kept on her desk and I cut the dress right below the waist.

"What are you doing?" Mabel said. "You don't have to change."

"It'll look better like this anyway," I said.

I pulled the jeans up and tucked in the fraying seam of what used to be a dress. I looked in the mirror and it was true—it looked better. And when we went back downstairs Javier complimented Mabel's new outfit and kissed her on the forehead while she muttered "whatever" and rolled her eyes. And Ana jumped up from her place on the sofa and took my hands.

"You look beautiful," she said. "Good choice."

I was buoyant with gratitude as we left the house. Mabel's parents called their reminders that we take a car home, not ride with our friends if they'd been drinking, not walk if it was after eleven. We called back our okays. I drifted down Guerrero Street, a girl with her best friend, a maker of good choices.

Too many people were at Ben's house. They crowded the foyer and the kitchen, made it difficult to hear anything anyone said to us. Mabel gestured to the kitchen, and I shook my head. It wasn't worth it. I caught a glimpse of Ben in the living room and grabbed Mabel's hand.

"Where's Laney?" I asked him when we were settled there on the soft green rug, the city lights through the windows, the nostalgia of everything taking me over. In seventh grade, Ben and I had spent a few months kissing each other until we realized we had more fun talking. I hadn't been in that room with him for a long time, but even with everyone else there, and the loudness of it, the way people were showing off for one another and getting wilder, I remembered our mellow afternoons, just him and me and the dog, once we discovered that we were meant to be just friends.

"I shut her in my parents' room," he said. "She gets nervous around too many people. You could go say hi to her, though, if you want. You remember where the treats are?"

"Yeah," I said. "I do."

It had been years, but I could picture the tin of dog treats on a shelf next to a stack of cookbooks. I wove my way past the groups of people and into the hall by the kitchen, and there was the tin, just as I'd remembered. Ben's parents' room was quiet, and Laney whimpered when I walked in. I closed the door behind me and sat on the carpet, fed her five treats, one after the next, the way we used to do when Ben and I were thirteen. I stayed in there, petting her head for a little bit longer, because it felt special to be somewhere other people weren't allowed to go.

When I got back to the living room and sat between Mabel and Ben, they were in the midst of a conversation with Courtney and a few other people. "We're basically the only teenagers in the city," a boy said. "All the private schools are worried because they're losing students every year."

Courtney said, "We might move."

"Whaaat?" Ben shook his head. "You've been my neighbor for, like, *ever*."

"I know. It's crazy. But I share a room with my brother, and it's not that cool anymore. When he was a little kid, fine. But now that he's hitting puberty? Not so much."

"Where would you go?" I asked her.

San Francisco always felt like an island to me, surrounded by the mythical East Bay with its restaurants and parks and North Bay with its wealth and its redwoods. South of the city was where our dead were buried—but not my mother, whose ashes returned to the ocean that killed her, which was also the ocean she loved. South of that were little beach towns, and then Silicon Valley and Stanford. But the people, everyone I knew, everyone I'd ever known, all lived in the city.

"Contra Costa," Courtney said.

"Gross," Ben said.

"You've probably never even been there."

"You're probably right."

"Snob!" Courtney punched his leg. "It's fine there. A lot of trees. I'm just so ready to have three bedrooms."

"We have three bedrooms. It can't be that hard to find. Maybe go out to the Sunset. That's where Marin lives."

"How big is your place?" Courtney asked me.

"It's a house," I said. "It's pretty big. I think three bedrooms."

"What do you mean, you *think*?"

"My grandpa lives in the back and I live in the front. I think there are two rooms back there. Maybe three."

Courtney's eyes narrowed.

"You haven't *been* in the back of your house?"

"It's not that weird," I said. "He has a study and a bedroom, but the bedroom opens up to something, either a big closet or a small room. I'm just not sure if it's technically a bedroom or not."

"Bedrooms have to have closets or else they aren't considered bedrooms," Eleanor, daughter of real-estate-agent parents, informed us.

"Oh," I said. "Then it's a three bedroom. It doesn't have a closet."

"It's probably a sitting room," Eleanor offered. "Lots of the old houses have them off the master bedrooms."

I nodded, but the truth is that I wasn't sure at all. I'd only caught glimpses through his study a couple times, but that's just how it was with us. I gave him his privacy and he gave me mine. Mabel would have loved that arrangement. Ana was always digging through her drawers.

But as the night got later, as people showed up and left, and the music got turned down because of the neighbors, and the alcohol flowed and then ran out, I kept seeing Courtney's look. Her narrowed eyes. The tone of her voice. *You haven't been in the back of your house?*

She was right. I hadn't been there.

I'd only paused in the doorway some nights when he was in his study, sitting at his desk, smoking his cigarettes, tapping the ash in his crystal ashtray and writing his letters by the light of an old-fashioned desk lamp, green with a bronze chain. Most of the time the door was shut but once in a while it was left open a crack, by mistake, probably.

Sometimes I'd call, "Good night," and he would say it back. But most of the time I walked quietly by, trying not to disturb him, until I got to our shared territory and then to my room, where nobody ever went besides Mabel and me.

"What's wrong?" Mabel asked me when we were back on the sidewalk, waiting for the car under a streetlamp. I shook my head. "Courtney was being kind of aggressive."

I shrugged. "It doesn't matter."

I was still thinking about Gramps at his desk. I was still wondering why I tried to be quiet when I walked past his rooms.

I was only giving him privacy. He was old, and the whites of his eyes seemed to grow more yellow every week, and he coughed like something was ready to rattle loose inside of him. A week ago I saw a red spot on his handkerchief when he lowered it from his mouth. He needed rest and quiet. He needed to save his strength. I was only being considerate. It's what anyone would do.

But still—doubts, doubts.

The car pulled up and we slid into the back. The driver eyed Mabel in the rearview mirror as she gave him her address.

He smiled, said something to her in Spanish, his tone so flirtatious I didn't need a translation.

She rolled her eyes.

"*México?*" he asked her.

"*Sí.*"

"*Colombia,*" he said.

"*One Hundred Years of Solitude* is one of my favorite books." I was embarrassed before the sentence was even finished. Just because he was from Colombia didn't mean that he'd care.

He adjusted the mirror and looked at me for the first time.

"You like García Márquez?"

"I love him. Do you?"

"*Love?* No. Admire? Yes." He turned right onto Valencia. A burst of laughter reached us from the sidewalk, still teeming with people.

"*Cien años de soledad,*" he said. "Your favorite? Really?"

"Is it that hard to believe?"

"Many people love that book. But you are so *young.*"

Mabel said something in Spanish. I slapped her leg and she grabbed my hand. Held it tight.

"I just said you were too smart for your own good," she said.

"Oh." I smiled at her. "Thanks."

"*Inteligente*, okay," he said. "Yes. But that is not why I ask."

"All the incest?" I asked.

"Ha! That, too. But no."

He pulled up to Mabel's house, and I wished he would circle the block. Mabel was pressed against me—she'd let go of my hand but we were still touching—and I didn't know why it felt so good but I knew I didn't want it to stop. And the driver was trying to tell me something about the book I'd read so many times. The one I kept discovering and trying to understand better. I wished he'd circle all night. Mabel's body and mine would relax into each other's. The car would fill with ideas about the passionate, tortured Buendía family, the once-grand city of Macondo, the way García Márquez wove magic into so many sentences.

But he put the car in park. He turned around to see me better.

"I do not mean the difficulty. I do not mean the sex. I mean there are too many failings. Not enough hope. Everything is despair. Everything is suffering. What I *mean* is don't be a person who seeks out grief. There is enough of that in life."

And then it was over—the car ride and the discussion, Mabel's body against mine—and we were letting ourselves into her garden and I was trying to call it back. The night was suddenly colder, and Courtney's voice was in my head again.

I wanted it out.

We climbed the stairs to Mabel's room and she shut the door.

"So was he right?" she asked me. "Are you the kind of person who seeks out grief? Or do you just like that book?"

"I don't know," I told her. "I don't think I'm that kind of person."

"I don't either," she said. "But it was an interesting thing to say."

I thought that it was more likely the opposite. I must have shut grief out. Found it in books. Cried over fiction instead of the truth. The truth was unconfined, unadorned. There was no poetic language to it, no yellow butterflies, no epic floods. There wasn't a town trapped underwater or generations of men with the same name destined to repeat the same mistakes. The truth was vast enough to drown in.

"You seem distracted," Mabel said.

"Just thirsty," I lied. "I'll get us water."

I walked barefoot down the stairs to the kitchen and flipped on the light. I crossed to the cabinet for the glasses and turned to fill them when I saw that on the island Ana had propped up her collage with a note in front of it that read, "*Gracias*, Marin. This was exactly what I needed."

Black satin, the remnants of my dress, now made waves at the bottom of the canvas. It was a black night, a black ocean. But the kitchen light sparked flecks of fool's gold stars, and out of the waves burst hand-painted shells, white and pink, the kind my mother loved.

I stared at it. Drank my glass of water and filled it up again. I kept looking for a long time, but I couldn't think of a single thing it might mean.

chapter eight

I UNDERSTAND what a New York winter storm is now. We are safely inside my room, but outside snow pours— not drifts—from the sky. The ground is disappearing. No more roads, no more paths. The tree branches are heavy and white, and Mabel and I are dorm-bound. It was good that we went out early, good we came back when we did.

It's only one, and we won't be going anywhere for a long time.

"I'm tired," Mabel says. "Or maybe it's just good napping weather."

I wonder if she's dreading the rest of the hours in this day. Maybe she wishes she hadn't come.

I think I'll close my eyes, too, try to sleep away the sick

feeling, the whisper that I am a waste of her time, her money, her effort.

But the whisper only gets louder. Mabel's breaths deepen and steady with sleep, and I am awake, mind swarming. I didn't answer her texts. I didn't return her calls or even listen to her voice mails. She came all the way to New York to invite me home with her, and I can't even tell her yes. *A waste, a waste.*

I lie like this for an hour, until I can't do it any longer.

I can make this better.

There is still time left.

When I get back to my room twenty minutes later, I'm carrying two plates of quesadillas, perfectly browned on both sides, topped with sour cream and salsa. I have two grapefruit sparkling waters nestled between my elbow and my ribs. I push open my door, grateful to see Mabel awake. She's sitting on Hannah's bed, staring out the window. Pure white. The whole world must be freezing.

As soon as she sees me, she jumps up to help with the plates and bottles.

"I woke up starving," she says.

"The stores here don't have *crema*," I say. "Hope sour cream is okay."

She takes a bite and nods her approval. We open our cans: a pop, a hiss. I try to determine what the feeling is between us at the moment, and hope that something has changed, that we could be, for a little while, at ease with each other. We eat in hungry silence, punctuated by a couple comments about the snow.

I wonder if we will become okay again. I hope for it.

Mabel crosses to the darkening window to look at my peperomia.

"There's pink on the edges of these leaves," she says. "I didn't notice before. Let's see how it looks in your new pot."

She reaches toward the bag from the pottery studio.

"Don't look!" I say. "There's something for you in there."

"What do you mean? I saw everything you bought!"

"Not *everything*," I say, grinning.

She's happy, impressed with me. She's looking at me the way she used to.

"I have something for you, too," she says. "But it's at home, so you'll have to come back with me to get it."

Without meaning to, I break our gaze.

"*Marin*," she says. "Is there something I don't know about? Some recently discovered family members? Some secret society or cult or something? Because as far as I know, you have no one. And I'm offering you something really huge and really *good*."

"I know. I'm sorry."

"I thought that you liked my parents."

"Of course I like them."

"Look at this," she says, picking up her phone. "My mom texted it to me. It was going to be a surprise."

She turns the screen toward me.

My name, painted in Ana's whimsical lettering on a door.

"My own room?"

"They redid the whole thing for you."

I know why she's angry. It should be so simple to say yes.

And I want to.

The walls of their guest room are vibrant blue, not a paint color but the pigment of the plaster itself. The wood floors are perfectly worn. You never have to worry about scratching them. I can imagine myself there, a permanent guest in my guest room, walking barefoot into the kitchen to pour myself mugs of coffee or glasses of water. I would help them make their delicious feasts, gather handfuls of sage and thyme from their front-porch herb garden.

I can imagine how it would look to live there, and I know the things I would do, but I can't feel it.

I can't say yes.

I have only just learned how to be here. Life is paper-thin and fragile. Any sudden change could rip it wide-open.

The swimming pool, certain shops on a certain street, Stop & Shop, this dorm, the buildings that house my classes—all of these are as safe as it gets, which is still not nearly safe enough.

When leaving campus, I never turn right because it

would take me too close to the motel. I can't fathom boarding a plane to San Francisco. It would be flying into ruins. But how could I begin to explain this to her? Even the good places are haunted. The thought of walking up her stairs to her front door, or onto the 31 bus, leaves me heavy with dread. I can't even think about my old house or Ocean Beach without panic thrumming through me.

"Hey," she says, voice soft. "Are you okay?"

I nod but I don't know if it's true.

The silence of my house. The food left, untouched, on the counter. The sharp panic of knowing I was alone.

"You're shaking," she says.

I need to swim. That plunge into water. That quiet. I close my eyes and try to feel it.

"Marin? What's going on?"

"I'm just trying . . . ," I say.

"Trying what?"

"Can you tell me something?"

"Sure."

"Anything. Tell me about one of your classes."

"Okay. I'm taking Art History? I think I might minor in it. I really love the Mexican art, which makes my mom so happy. Like Frida Kahlo. Her paintings are so . . . *strong*. There are all the self-portraits, close-ups of her face and shoulders with variations. Like sometimes she has animals with her, monkeys, a weird hairless dog, that kind of thing. And some are more simple. Is this right? Am I helping?"

I nod.

"My current favorite is called *The Two Fridas*. It's pretty much the way it sounds. There are two versions of her, sitting next to each other on a bench. One is wearing a long white dress with an elaborate lace bodice and collar, and the other one is dressed in . . . I don't remember exactly. Something more relaxed. But the thing that I really like about it is you can see their hearts. You can see right into their chests. Or maybe their hearts are outside their chests. It's kind of gruesome, like most of her paintings, but it's also really dramatic and beautiful."

"I'd like to see it."

"I can pull it up if you want me to. Hold on one second."

I open my eyes.

We are in my room.

My hands are still.

She's taking my computer off my desk and entering a search. She sits down next to me and positions the screen between us, resting it on one of my knees and one of hers. The painting is how she described it, but there's also more. Behind the two Fridas are storm clouds, gray-blue and white.

"I can't tell," I say, "if the trouble is coming or if it's passed and already left them."

"Or maybe they're in the middle of it," she says. "Something is happening with the hearts."

The hearts are connected by a thin red line. A vein. It's bleeding onto the Frida in the white dress, who is holding a pair of scissors. I point to her heart.

"We're looking inside her chest to see it," I say. "And it looks painful. But the other one . . ." I point to her. "I think her heart's outside her body. It's still whole."

"You're right," Mabel says.

Where the one in the white dress has scissors, this one has something else.

"What is she holding?"

"It's a tiny portrait of Diego Rivera. She painted this during their divorce."

"So it's about losing him," I say.

"Yeah, I guess," she says. "That's what my professor says. But doesn't that make it too simple?"

I turn my head to look at Mabel.

"It's better if it's complicated?" I say.

She smiles. "Well, obviously."

I take another look at the screen. "Maybe it really *is* as simple as it looks, though. She was one person before. She had a whole heart and the man she loved. She was at ease. And then something happened, and it changed her. And now she's wounded."

"Are you trying to tell me something?" Mabel says. "Are

you finally answering me? If you need to do it this way, I'd be happy to find a bunch of paintings for you to analyze."

"No," I say. "I mean, yes—I know how she feels. But that's not what I'm doing. I'm just looking at your painting."

"The thing I most love about it," Mabel says, "is how they're holding hands right at the center of the painting. It's so important. It's what the whole thing's about, I think."

"It could mean so many different things."

"Like what? I just think it means the Fridas are still connected. Even though she's changed, she's still the same person."

"Yeah, it could mean that," I say. "But it could also be something else. Like the whole one is trying to pull the wounded one back to her, as if she could undo what's happened. Or the wounded one is guiding her old self into her new life. Or it could be that they've separated almost entirely from each other, and they are holding hands as a last moment of connection before they break apart completely."

Mabel stares at the image.

"And *why* are you changing your major?" she asks.

"Because wouldn't it be better," I say, "if the hand-holding really just meant they were connected, and you didn't have to think about the other possibilities?"

"No," she says. "Not at all. That would not—*in any way*—be better than realizing that there are many ways to see one thing. I love this painting even more now."

She sets the computer down on the bed. She stands up and glares down at me.

"Seriously," she says. "*Natural Sciences?*"

And then everything goes dark.

chapter nine

WE DECIDE WE SHOULDN'T WORRY because, even though it's cold and getting colder in here, we have jackets and blankets. If it comes to it, we can pick locks and scavenge for candles. For now, we have a few tea lights from Hannah's drawer.

Our cell phones still have some charge left, but we're using them sparingly and there's no Wi-Fi anyway.

"Remember when the power went out sophomore year?" Mabel asks.

"I made you listen to me read all night."

"Sylvia Plath and Anne Sexton."

"Right. Those were dark poems."

"Yeah, but they were fun, too."

"They were defiant," I say. I remember the sparks in them, I remember how the words made me feel dangerous and strong. "Lady Lazarus" and "Daddy" and all of Anne Sexton's reimagined fairy tales.

"In my lit class we listened to a recording of Sylvia Plath. Her voice wasn't what I thought it would sound like."

I know those recordings. I used to listen to them online sometimes late at night. Every word she spoke was a dagger.

"What did you think she'd sound like?" I ask her.

She shrugs. "Like you, I guess."

We drift into silence. The colder it gets, the more difficult it is not to worry. What if we can't pick locks? What if the electricity doesn't come back on for days? What if we get too cold while sleeping and don't wake up in time to save ourselves?

"Maybe we should turn our phones off," I say. "In case we need them later."

Mabel nods. She looks at her phone, and I wonder if she's thinking about calling Jacob before she turns it off. The light of the screen casts across her face, but I can't read her expression. Then she holds down a button and her face goes dark again.

I cross the room to look for mine. I don't keep it near me all the time the way she does or the way I used to. I don't get many texts or calls. I find it next to the bag of Claudia's pottery. I pick it up, but before I can power it off it buzzes.

"Who is it?" Mabel asks.

"I don't know," I say. "An area code from here."

"You should answer it."

"Hello?"

"Don't know how long you were planning on sticking it out," a man says. "But I imagine it's getting to be pretty chilly in there. And it looks mighty dark."

I turn to the window. The groundskeeper is standing in the snow. I can barely see him but for the headlights of his truck.

"Mabel," I whisper. She looks up from her phone and joins me at the window.

I pick up one of the tea lights and wave it in front of the window, a tiny hello I'm not sure he can see from there. He lifts his hand in a wave.

"The power's out for you, too, though. Isn't it?" I ask.

"Yes," he says. "But I don't live in a dormitory."

We blow out the candles. We pull on our boots and grab our toothbrushes. And then we are out in the impossible cold, leaving trails of footprints in the snow from the dorm entrance to where his truck is idling.

He's younger up close. Not *young*, but not old either.

"Tommy," he says. He sticks out his hand and I shake it.

"Marin," I say.

"Mabel."

"Marin. Mabel. You're in luck, because there's a fireplace in my living room and also a fold-out couch."

Even though I'm glad to hear this, it doesn't hit me until after we step inside his little cottage on the edge of the grounds that this is what we needed. I'd gotten so cold I almost forgot what it felt like to be warm enough. His fireplace is crackling and bright, casting light across the ceiling and the walls.

"I've got the oven on, too. This old thing could heat the house on its own—just be careful not to touch it."

All the walls are wood paneled, and everything is worn in and soft. Rugs upon rugs, sofas and overstuffed chairs, all of them strewn with blankets. He doesn't offer to show us around, but it's a small space and we can see most of it from where we stand, waiting for him to show us whether we'll spend the evening making small talk or if he'll say good night and retreat to the door at the end of the short hallway.

"It's just six thirty," Tommy says. "I assume you didn't eat."

"We had some food a couple hours ago," I say. "But no dinner yet."

"I'm not big on dinner myself, but I have some pasta and a jar of sauce. . . ."

He shows us how to light the burner with a match on his old-fashioned stove and fills a heavy silver pot with water. He keeps his spaghetti in a canister; there isn't much inside.

"As I said, I'm not too big on dinner. Hopefully this'll be enough for the two of you."

I can't tell if he's lying. I should have thought about all the food in the dorm refrigerator before we left, but I can't fathom going back out into the snow and the dark, walking all that way.

"Are you sure?" Mabel asks. "We could make it work for all of us. We don't need that much."

"No, no, I'm sure." He takes a look in the canister again and frowns. Then he opens his freezer. "Jackpot!" He pulls out a bag of frozen dinner rolls.

"And the oven's already preheated," I say.

"Meant to be. I'm going to have a couple rolls and some slices of cheese. You'll have pasta and the rest of the rolls and whatever else you see that pleases you."

He opens the refrigerator so we can take a look. There isn't much inside of it, but it's clean and neatly arranged.

"Sounds great," Mabel says, but I just nod.

This is the first time I've been in a home since leaving mine, and my eyes are adjusting to the dark, and every new thing I make out fills me with wonder.

A few dishes are in his sink; a pair of slippers rest by the doorway. The freezer has three photographs on it—a little boy, Tommy with some friends, a man in a military uniform. Books are strewn across the coffee table along with two video-game controllers.

Nothing in his refrigerator is labeled. Everything here is his own.

There was a blue-and-gold blanket that lived on Gramps's recliner in the living room for my entire life. I spent so many winter hours nestled under it, reading my books, drifting to sleep. It was almost threadbare in some places, but it still brought me warmth.

I don't know where it is now.

I want it.

"Marin," Tommy says. "I needed to get ahold of you anyway. I'm heading off campus for Christmas and will likely be spending the night away. I'll be with some friends in Beacon. Call me if anything goes wrong, and here are the numbers for the police and the fire station. Call these direct lines, not nine-one-one."

"Okay. Thank you," I say, careful not to look at Mabel. I wish I could ask if she knows what happened to all of our things. Did anyone save anything? Did they wonder where I was?

Ana and Javier. They waited in the police station for me. Where did they go next, once they discovered I was gone? The looks that must have been on their faces—I don't even want to imagine it.

Why *won't* I just say yes? Why won't I fly home to them and apologize for my disappearing act and accept their forgiveness when they offer it and sleep in the bed they made for me in the room with my name on the door?

If I could undo that decision in the police station, I

wouldn't have left through the back. The two weeks in the motel would never have happened and the thought of diner coffee wouldn't make me choke.

Tommy's putting the frozen rolls in the oven. He's sparking the flame of a burner using a match, saying, "Good thing it's gas," and Mabel is nodding yes and I am, too.

But I'm not hungry.

"I'm still feeling really cold for some reason," I say. "I'm just going to sit by the fire if that's okay."

"Be my guest. As soon as these rolls are done I'm going to head to the back and you guys can make yourselves comfortable. I've got some presents to wrap and I was just waiting for an excuse to go to bed early. Power outage'll do it."

So I drift to an armchair and I look at the fire. And I think of all of these things from what used to be my home.

The blanket.

The copper pots, passed down from Gramps's mother.

The round kitchen table and the rectangular dining table.

The chairs with their threadbare cushions and wicker backs.

My grandmother's china, covered in tiny red flowers.

The mismatched mugs, the delicate teacups, the tiny spoons.

The wooden clock with its loud *tick-tick-tick* and the oil painting of the village Gramps was from.

The hand-tinted photographs in the hallway, the needlepoint pillows on the sofa, the ever-changing grocery list stuck to the refrigerator under a magnet in the shape of a Boston terrier.

The blanket, again, blue and gold and soft.

And now Tommy is saying good night and walking down the hallway, and Mabel is in the living room with me, setting small bowls of pasta onto the coffee table and lowering herself to the floor.

I eat without tasting anything. I eat even though I don't know if I'm hungry.

IT WAS A COUPLE WEEKS after the night at Ben's and the Colombian driver, and Mabel and I decided to sneak out on our own. Ana and Javier always stayed up late, sometimes into the early morning, so I fell asleep a little after ten knowing that my phone would buzz hours later to announce her arrival and I'd slip out then.

Gramps cooked dinner at six o'clock most nights. We usually ate in the kitchen unless he made something fancy, in which case he'd tell me to set the dining room table, and we'd eat with shiny brass candlesticks between us. After dinner he washed and I dried until the kitchen was as clean as it could be given its age and constant use, and then Gramps drifted off to his back rooms to smoke cigarettes and write letters and read.

My phone buzzed and I left quietly, not knowing whether I was breaking a rule. It's possible that Gramps would have been fine with Mabel and me going to the beach at night to sit and watch the waves and talk. I could have asked him, but we didn't work that way.

Mabel was on the sidewalk, her dark hair spilling from under a knit cap, her hands in fingerless gloves clasped together. I had a parka zipped over my sweater.

"You're all bundled up," she said. "How am I going to offer to help keep you warm?"

We laughed.

"I can ditch it if you want, baby," I joked.

"Why don't you run upstairs, get rid of that jacket, and come back with some of Gramps's whiskey."

"Actually, the whiskey's not a bad idea."

I let myself back in and crossed the living room, slipped through the open pocket doors to the dining room, and grabbed the bottle of whiskey that lived on the built-in hutch.

Then I was back on the street, stuffing the bottle under my jacket. Two girls walking to the beach at night was one thing. Add an open and visible bottle, and we'd be inviting the cops to stop us.

It was almost three in the morning and the city was still. Not a single car passed us all four blocks to the beach. We didn't have to bother with crosswalks. We stepped straight from the street to the sand, scaled a dune, and then found ourselves near the edge of the black water. I was waiting for my eyes to adjust to the dark, but it wasn't happening, so eventually I had to give in to it.

"Remember how we used to practice kissing?" I asked, pulling the top off the whiskey.

"We were determined to be experts by the time we were sophomores."

"Experts," I said, laughing. I took a sip, and the burn of it surprised me. We were used to pilfered beers or vodka mixed with whatever juice was in our friends' pantries. "Here, drink at your own peril," I rasped.

Mabel took a sip, coughed.

"We were so giggly and nervous," I said, remembering us as freshmen. "We had no idea what it meant to be in high school. What we were supposed to act like, what we were supposed to talk about . . ."

"It was so much fun."

"What was?"

"All of it. Let me have another try with that." Her hand felt around in the dark for the bottle, and then she found it and I let go. She tipped her face toward the hazy moon. Handed the bottle back. I took a swig.

"Better this time," she said, and she was right. And with

each subsequent sip it got easier to swallow, and soon my body felt heavy and my head swam, and everything Mabel said made me laugh and every memory I had was meaningful.

We were quiet then, for a little while, until she sat up.

"It's been a long time since we practiced," she said, crawling toward me until our noses touched. A laugh started in my throat, but then she put her mouth on mine.

Wet lips.

Soft tongue.

Her legs wrapped around my waist and we kissed harder. Soon we were lying in the sand, her salt-thick, tangled hair through my fingers.

She unzipped my parka. Her cold hands found their way under my sweater as she kissed my neck.

"What would Sister Josephine say?" I whispered.

I felt her smile against my collarbone.

It took her a couple tries to get my bra unclasped with one hand, but when she did, the cold air against my skin was nothing compared to the warmth of her breath. I unbuttoned her sweater, pushed her bra over her breasts without unfastening it. I had never felt so ravenous. It's not like my experience was vast. It's not like I was used to being touched this way. But even if I had already been kissed by dozens of mouths, I would have known this was different.

I loved her already.

With our jeans unfastened, Mabel's fingers grazing the elastic of my underwear, she said, "If we regret this tomorrow, we can blame it on the whiskey."

But the sky was fading from black to gray; it was already tomorrow. And I didn't regret anything.

We opened our eyes to the morning fog, a flock of sanderlings darting across the sky. Mabel's hand was in mine and I was looking at her fingers, smaller than mine and a few shades darker, and I wanted them under my clothes again but didn't dare say it.

Without the darkness we felt exposed, and the early-morning commuters were already heading to work. The overnight shifters were finally off. We had to wait at every crosswalk.

"What are they all thinking of us?" I asked.

"Well, we're clearly not homeless. Your jacket's too nice."

"And we did not just roll out of bed."

"Right," she said. "Because we are covered in sand."

The light changed and we crossed the Great Highway.

"Maybe they think we're beach creatures," I said.

"Mermaids?"

"We're missing the tails."

"Maybe they think we're scavengers, up early to comb the sand."

"Yes," I said. "Like you probably have a few gold watches in your pockets, and I have some wedding bands and rolls of cash."

"Perfect."

I was aware of how our voices were a little higher pitched than usual, our words rushed. I was aware of how we hadn't looked into each other's faces since we stood up and dusted the sand off our clothes. Of the sand that still clung to my skin and the scent of Mabel everywhere.

Gramps spotted us before I saw him. He was waving at us from across the street with one arm, pulling the garbage bin out to the curb with the other.

"Hello, girls!" he shouted, as though it were a pleasant surprise to see us out this early.

We didn't know what to say as we walked toward him.

"Morning, Gramps," I finally mustered, but by then his expression had changed.

"My whiskey."

I followed his gaze. I hadn't even realized Mabel was carrying it like that, by its neck, totally exposed.

He could have looked at us and seen our kiss-swollen lips and blushing faces. Could have seen how neither of us could look him—or each other—in the eye. But he was looking at the bottle instead.

"Sorry, Gramps," I said. "We only took a few swigs."

"We're lightweights," Mabel tried to joke, but her voice was thick with regret.

He reached out and she surrendered the bottle. He held it eye level to get a good look at how much was inside.

"It's okay," he said. "It was only a little."

"I'm really sorry," Mabel said.

I wished I were back on the beach with her. I willed the sky to turn dark again.

"Gotta be careful with this stuff," Gramps said. "Best not to get involved with it at all."

I nodded, trying to remember kissing Mabel's mouth.

I wanted her to look at me.

"I have to get home," she said.

"Have a good day at school," Gramps told her.

"Thanks."

She was standing on the sidewalk in torn-up jeans and a sweater, her dark hair falling to one side, so long it grazed her elbow. Her brow was furrowed and her eyes were sad until she caught me, finally looking, and she smiled.

"I hope you don't get in trouble," I said, but how could trouble find us?

We were miraculous.

We were beach creatures.

We had treasures in our pockets and each other on our skin.

chapter eleven

ABOVE ME IS the head and neck of a deer. A buck, I guess.
His antlers cast long and graceful shadows along the wall.
I imagine him alive, in a field somewhere. I think about
spring, grass and flowers, hoofprints and movement and a
body, intact. But now there is stillness and drips of candle
wax and quiet. There are the ghosts of who we used to be.
There is the *clink* of Mabel setting our dinner bowls into
Tommy's sink, and the exhaustion that comes with knowing
that something will have to happen next, and then after that,
and on and on until it's over.

We haven't talked about sleeping yet. On the sofa are a
set of sheets and a comforter, a reminder of the space we are
supposed to share.

Maybe we'll stay up all night.

Mabel returns from the kitchen. She crosses to the bookshelf and picks up a deck of cards.

She turns to show me, and I nod. She shuffles and deals ten for me, ten for herself, places a card faceup. Queen of spades. I can't believe I didn't buy a deck of cards for us. It would have answered the question of what to do each time it came up. We wouldn't have had to trick ourselves into sleep to stave off the need for conversation.

We dive into gin rummy as though no time had passed. I finish the first round ahead twelve points, and Mabel gets up to find us a pencil and paper. She comes back with a Sharpie and a postcard mailer for a Christmas tree lot. *Nothing beats the smell of fresh-cut pine,* it says, and below the sentence are photographs of three types of fir trees: Douglas, noble, and grand. Mabel writes our names below a P.S.—*We have wreaths, too!*—and adds the score.

It's a close game, which means it's a long one, and by our last hand my vision keeps blurring from tiredness and the strain of seeing in the dark. Mabel keeps losing track of whose turn it is, even though there are only two of us, but in the end she calls gin and wins the game.

"Nice job," I say, and she smiles.

"I'm gonna get ready for bed."

The whole time she's gone I don't move. Maybe she

wanted me to pull out the bed, but I'm not going to do it. It's a decision we have to make together.

She comes back a few minutes later.

"Careful," she says. "Some candles burned out. It's really dark back there."

"Okay," I say. "Thanks."

I wait for her to do or say something.

Finally, I ask, "So should we get the bed ready?"

Even in the dark, I can see her concern.

"Do you see other options?" I ask her. There are only a couple of chairs and the floor.

"That rug is pretty soft," she says.

"If that's what you want."

"It isn't what I *want*. It's just . . ."

"He doesn't have to know. And it's only sleeping, anyway." I shake my head. After everything, this is so stupid. "How many times did we sleep in the same bed before anything happened? Hundreds? I think we'll be okay tonight."

"I know."

"I promise not to mess anything up for you."

"Marin, come on."

"It's your call," I say. "I don't really want to sleep on the rug. But if you don't want to share the bed I can sleep on the couch without pulling it out so you can have more room. Or maybe we could push two chairs together or something."

She's quiet. I can see that she's thinking, so I give her a minute.

"You're right," she finally says. "I'm sorry. Let's just get the bed ready."

"You don't have to be sorry," I mutter.

And now I'm taking the cushions off the sofa, and Mabel is moving the coffee table to the side of the room to make space for the bed to fold out. We find handles on each side and pull. Squeaky bedsprings, flimsy mattress. She shakes out the fitted sheet and we put it on together, tuck in the sides because the mattress is so thin.

"The rug's looking better and better," I say.

"Getting cold feet?"

I feel myself smile, and when I look at her she's smiling back at me already.

"I can do the rest," she says, picking up a pillowcase. "You go get ready."

Like Jane Eyre, I carry a candle to light my way. But when I get to the bathroom and look in the mirror, all I see is myself. Despite the darkness, the long shadows, the quiet, this room is free of intruders and ghosts. I splash icy water on my face, dry it with a towel Tommy left out for us. I brush my teeth, I pee, I wash my hands, and pull my hair back in a rubber band I brought with me. I think of Jane Eyre with Mr. Rochester, of how much she loved him and how certain she was that they could never be together, and I think of how in a couple of minutes I'll be in bed with Mabel. I tried to make it sound like it was nothing, but it is something—I know that. She knows it.

Maybe her hesitation wasn't about Jacob at all. It could just have been over the ways we've changed. It could be that she's still too angry to think about the weight of my body on the same mattress, the accidental contact we'll make throughout the night when we're too lost in sleep to keep to one side or the other.

I take the candle and head back to the living room. She's already in bed, on her side facing the edge. I can't see her face but I think her eyes are closed. I climb onto the other side. The springs groan. No sense in pretending she could sleep through the noise of it.

"*Good night*," I whisper.

"Good night," she says.

Our backs are to each other's. We're as far apart as two people could be on a mattress this size. The space between us is worse than our awkwardness, worse than not knowing what she's thinking during our long stretches of silence.

I think I hear something.

I think she's crying.

And here are things I'd forgotten, resurfacing. Text messages she sent.

Did you meet someone?

You can tell me if you did.

I just need to know.

There were others, too, but I can't remember them. In the beginning her texts were knives, slicing holes in the cocoon of motel must and diner coffee and the view of the street out my window. But after school started, after Hannah, I was a stranger with a secondhand phone and someone named Mabel had the wrong number.

That girl she was trying to reach—she must have been running from something. She must have been someone special, for her friend to keep trying so hard. Too bad she was gone now.

We never talked about what would happen to us.

That was another one.

The way we used to kiss. How I would catch her looking at me from across the room. Her grin, my blush. Her thigh, soft, against my cheek. I had to deny all of it, because it was part of a life that was over.

All I can hear is the crackle of the fire. She may not have really been crying—I may have imagined it—but I can feel it now, the way I hurt her. Maybe it's all of this remembering or talking about books and paintings again or being with Mabel, but I can feel the ghost of me creeping back. *Remember me?* she's asking.

I think I do.

And that girl would have comforted Mabel. She would have touched her as though a touch were something simple. So I lift my hand, search for a safe place on Mabel's body. Her shoulder. I touch her there, and before I have time to wonder if it's unwanted, Mabel's hand covers mine, holding it in place.

chapter twelve

LATER THAT DAY, after Gramps had caught us with the whiskey and Mabel and I had spent the school hours blushing every time we saw each other, after Gramps had made a casserole for dinner and there had been more quiet between us than usual, he asked me to sit down on the love seat.

I nodded.

"Sure," I said, but my chest filled with ice.

I didn't know how I'd answer the questions he was about to ask me. Everything was too new. I followed him into the living room and took my seat. He stood in front of me, towering, not even a hint of a smile, only worry and sadness and something verging on panic.

"Listen," he said. "I want to tell you about different kinds of love."

I braced myself for his disapproval. I had rarely felt it before, and never for anything substantial. And I braced myself, too, for my anger. Because as unexpected as Mabel's kiss had been, and as nervous and unsettled as I'd felt ever since, I knew that what we did wasn't wrong.

"You may have gotten the wrong impression," he continued. "About Birdie and me. It isn't like that between us."

I felt a laugh escape me. It was out of relief, but he didn't take it that way.

"It may be difficult to believe," he said. "I know it may have come across as . . . *romantic*, because of how I act when I get her letters. Because of that dress she sent me. But sometimes two people have a deep connection. It makes romance seem trivial. It isn't about anything carnal. It's about souls. About the deepest part of who you are as a person."

He seemed so worried, so nervous. All of my relief slipped away, and concern replaced it.

"Okay, Gramps," I said. "Whatever it is, I'm glad that you have her."

He took his handkerchief out of his pocket and carefully unfolded it. He patted his forehead, his upper lip. I had never seen him so worked up about anything.

"Really," I said. "Don't worry about what I think. I just want you to be happy."

"Sailor," he said. "If I didn't have her, I would be lost."

I wasn't enough of a companion. I wasn't any kind of

anchor. I felt the blow of it but I swallowed the hurt and said, "I'm sure she feels the same for you."

He studied my face. It felt like he was looking through me to something else. He nodded, slowly.

"It's true. Maybe even more so," he said. "I need her and she needs me. Boy, does she need me."

Maybe he was going to say more, but the doorbell rang, the card game was about to begin, so I got up and went down to open the gate. Usually I would clear the kitchen when they came, but I was afraid that something was wrong with Gramps. I wanted to know that he was back to himself. I finished drying the dishes on the rack as they poured their first drinks and started to play. Then I left for a while but couldn't stop worrying, so I went back to make myself tea.

As the water heated up, I saw Jones take Gramps's bottle, pour a little more into his glass.

Gramps eyed the glass, then eyed Jones.

"What's that for?"

"You were empty."

Jones glanced at the other two. Freeman was shuffling more times than necessary, but Bo met Jones's eyes.

"No need to hurry me up," Gramps said. "I'm getting there fine on my own." His voice was low, almost a growl.

Bo shook his head. Something was a shame, but I didn't know what.

Jones cleared his throat. He swallowed.

"It's just a drink, Delaney," he finally said.

Gramps looked up at Jones, his eyes fierce, for the entire time that Freeman dealt the cards. The other guys picked up their hands, putting what they received in order, but Gramps just stared, daring Jones to look back.

I didn't know what was happening, but I wanted it to end.

"Gramps?" I said.

He jerked toward me as though he'd forgotten I was there.

"I was wondering . . . ," I said, not knowing where my sentence would end. "Maybe . . . Will you drive me to school tomorrow? I might feel like sleeping in."

"Sure, Sailor," he said.

He turned back to the table. He picked up his cards. Everyone was quiet, no heckling, not a single joke.

"I'll bet five," Gramps said.

Jones folded.

I went back into my room with the tea and tried to forget.

Mabel and I texted for hours. We didn't make plans to sneak out and meet. We didn't even talk. Hearing the other's voice would have been bright and dangerous, so instead we tapped out messages.

What were we thinking?

I don't know.

Did you like it?

Yes.

Me too.

We texted about a song we liked and some random YouTube videos, about a poem we read in English that day, and what we would do if we were faced with the end of the world. We texted about Mabel's uncle and his husband, who lived on three acres in New Mexico, and how we would make our way there, build a hut, and dig a well and grow our food and make the most of what time we had left.

The end of the world never sounded so good.

I know!

I kind of want it to happen. Is that bad?

We could do all that stuff even without the apocalypse.

Good point.

So it's a plan?

Yes.

It was almost two a.m. by the time we said good night. I smiled into my pillow, closed my eyes, wished for the feeling to last. I saw our futures unfolding, all pink clouds and cacti and bright sun and forever.

And then I got up and went to the kitchen for water. I filled the glass and gulped it down, then headed toward the bathroom. The door to Gramps's room was ajar. Light was shining through the narrow space. I walked softly past it and then I heard something rustle and turned back. Gramps was at his desk, his brass lamp burning, his pen moving furiously across his paper. I was quiet, but I could tell—I could have called his name and he wouldn't have looked up. I could have banged the pots and pans together.

He was writing his love letters, I told myself, but it didn't look like love.

He finished a page and cast it aside, started a next one. He was hunched forward and furious. I turned toward the bathroom and locked the door behind me.

He was only writing love letters, I thought.

Only love letters. Love letters.

chapter thirteen

IN THE STILLNESS of this unfamiliar living room, another
memory surfaces.

A couple nights after graduation, we all met on Ocean
Beach. Everyone was acting wild, like it was the end of everything. Like we'd never see one another again, and maybe,
in some cases, that was true.

I found Mabel and joined her on a blanket just in time
to hear the punch line of a joke I already knew. I smiled
while everybody laughed, and she looked so beautiful in the
bonfire glow.

We *all* looked so beautiful.

I could say the night felt magical, but that would be em-
bellishment. That would be romanticization. What it actually felt like was life. We weren't thinking of what would
happen next. No one talked about the way the summer was

supposed to unfold or the places we'd find ourselves in the fall. It was as if we had made a pact to be in the moment, or like being in the moment was the only way to be. Telling jokes, telling secrets. Ben had his guitar and for a while he played and we just listened as the fire sparked and the waves crashed and subsided. I felt something on my hand. Mabel's finger, tracing my knuckles. She slipped her thumb under my palm. I could have kissed her, but I didn't.

Now, her hand on mine after so long apart, here in Tommy's house and nowhere close to sleep, I wonder what might have changed if I had. If one of us had made the fact of us common knowledge, we would have become something to be discussed and decided upon. Maybe there would have been no Jacob. Maybe her photograph would be on my bulletin board. Maybe we wouldn't be here now, and I would be in California in her parents' orange-walled living room, sipping hot chocolate by the Christmas tree.

But probably not. Because even though it was only a couple months later that Gramps left me, when I tried to call back that night it no longer felt like life.

When I think of all of us then, I see how we were in danger. Not because of the drinking or the sex or the hour of the night. But because we were so innocent and we didn't even know it. There's no way of getting it back. The confidence. The easy laughter. The sensation of having left home only for a little while. Of having a home to return to.

We were innocent enough to think that our lives were what we thought they were, that if we pieced all of the facts about ourselves together they'd form an image that made sense—that looked like us when we looked in the mirror, that looked like our living rooms and our kitchens and the people who raised us—instead of revealing all the things we didn't know.

Mabel lets go of my hand and kicks back the covers. She sits up, so I do the same.

"I guess I'm not ready to fall asleep yet," she says.

It's so warm now that I'm glad to have the covers off. We sit on the bed and lean against the cushioned back of the sofa. We're watching the firelight flicker across the room, and Mabel is pulling her hair back, twisting it in circles and then letting it go, and I feel like the night might last forever and I would be okay with that.

"Where did you stay when you got here? I mean before the dorms. It's something I've been wondering."

I didn't expect this, but I want to give her the answer. I take a long look at the ceiling and I nod in case she's watching me. I need a moment to steady my heart so I can speak. By the time I look back she's shifted. Her head is resting on her hand and she's watching me with a look I don't know if I've ever seen on her before. She's so still and so patient.

"I found a motel."

"Close by?"

"Sort of. I think it was like twenty minutes away. I got on a bus from the airport and I rode the line until I saw a place out the window."

"What was it like?"

"Not nice."

"Why did you stay?"

"I guess it never occurred to me that I could leave."

I think about walking into the room, the way it smelled—worse than stale, worse than unclean. I thought I might be able to exist there without touching anything, but then hours passed and it turned out I was wrong.

"It was a hotel where people live when they don't have anywhere else to go," I tell Mabel. "Not a place where people stay on vacation." I pull the blanket over me, even though I'm not cold. "It scared me. But I was already scared."

"That's not what I pictured."

"What did you think?"

"I thought maybe you got to move into the dorms early or something. Did you meet people?"

"At the motel?"

She nods.

"I wouldn't say that I *met* people. I had a lot of neighbors. Some of them became familiar."

"I mean did you hang out with them?"

"No."

"I thought you must have met people."

I shake my head.

"I thought they were helping you through everything."

"No," I say. "I was alone there."

In her face something is shifting. A set of facts to replace all the guessing I made her do. I want to give her more.

"There was a woman next door to me who howled," I say. "At cars that went by, at people who passed. After I checked into my room she howled for a few straight hours."

"What was wrong with her?"

"I don't know. She sounded like a wolf. I kept wondering then—I'm still wondering now—if there was a time when she realized that something was going wrong. Inside her, I mean. When she could feel herself slipping away, something new creeping in. If she could have stopped it, or if it just . . . *happened*. It made me think about *Jane Eyre*. Remember?"

"The crazy woman. Mr. Rochester's first wife."

"I felt like Jane when she sees her in the mirror. I was afraid. I'd listen to her at night and sometimes I felt like I understood what she was trying to say. I was afraid I'd turn into her."

The fact of her was scary enough, but the fact of me, in an identical room, just as alone as she was, that was the worst part. There was only a wall between us, and it was so thin it was almost nothing. Jane, too, was once locked up in a room with a ghost. It was terrifying, the idea that we could fall asleep girls, minty breathed and nightgowned, and wake to find ourselves wolves.

"I can see why you don't want to read much right now."

I nod. "Before, they were just stories. But now, they keep swarming back, and all of them feel more terrible."

She looks away and I wonder if it's because I'm telling her things she can't relate to. Maybe she thinks I'm being dramatic. Maybe I am. But I know that there's a difference between how I used to understand things and how I do now. I used to cry over a story and then close the book, and it all would be over. Now everything resonates, sticks like a splinter, festers.

"You were alone," she says. "For all those days."

"Does that change anything?"

She shrugs.

"You thought I met new people and didn't need you?"

"It was the only explanation I could think of."

I will tell her anything as long as she keeps asking questions. It's the darkness and the warmth. The feeling of being in someone else's home, in neutral territory, nothing mine and nothing hers, no clues about each other in the blankets or the firewood or the photographs on the mantel.

It makes my life feel far away, even though I'm right here.

"What else do you want to know?" I ask her.

"I've been wondering about Birdie."

She shifts, and the springs pop and settle. My hands lie

heavy in my lap. Her face is still watchful and willing. I can still breathe.

"Okay," I say. "What about Birdie?"

"Does she know what happened? No one was there to check the mail and find her letters. By now, they'd all be sent back, and I keep wondering if anyone told her that he died."

"There was no Birdie," I say.

Confusion flashes across her face.

I wait for the next question.

"But, the letters . . ."

Ask me.

"I guess . . . ," she says. "I guess it was too sweet of a story. All of those love letters to someone he never even met. I guess . . . ," she says again. "He must have been really lonely to make something like that up."

She won't meet my eyes. She doesn't want me to tell her anything more, at least not right now. I know what it's like to not want to understand, so we're quiet while her last sentence spins and spins in my head. And I think, *I was lonely.* I *was.* Touching knees under the table wasn't enough. Love-seat lectures were not enough. Sugary things, cups of coffee, rides to school were not enough.

An ache expands in my chest.

"He didn't need to be lonely."

Mabel's brow furrows.

"I was there. He had me, but he wrote letters instead."

She finally looks at me again.

"*I* was lonely," I say.

And then I say it again, because I told myself lies for so long, and now my body is still and my breath is steady and I feel alive with the truth.

Before I know what's happening, Mabel is pulling me close. I think I remember what this feels like. I try not to think of the last time we held each other, which was the last time I was held by anybody. Her arms are around me so tight that I can't even hug her back, so I rest my head on her shoulder and I try to stay still so that she won't let go.

"*Let's sleep*," she whispers into my ear, and I nod, and we break apart and lie down again.

I face away from her for a long time so that she won't see my sadness. To be held like that, to be let go. But then the ghost of me starts whispering again. She's reminding me of how cold I've been. How I've been freezing. She's saying that Mabel's warm and that she loves me. Maybe a love that's different than it used to be, but love all the same. The ghost of me is saying, *Three thousand miles. That's how much she cares.* She's telling me it's okay.

So I turn over and find Mabel closer to me than I'd realized. I wait a minute there to see if she'll move away, but she doesn't. I wrap my arm around her waist, and she relaxes into me. My head nestles in the curve behind her neck; my knees pull up to fit the space behind hers.

She might be asleep. I'll only stay here for a couple of minutes. Only until I thaw completely. Until it's enough to remind me what it feels like to be close to another person, enough to last me for another span of months. I breathe her in. Tell myself I need to turn away.

Soon. But not yet.

"Don't disappear again," she says. "Okay?"

Her hair is soft against my face.

"Promise me."

"I promise."

I start to turn, but she reaches back for my arm. She scoots her body closer into mine, until the full lengths of us are touching. With each breath, I feel winter passing.

I close my eyes, and I breathe her in, and I think about this home that belongs to neither of us, and I listen to the fire crackling, and I feel the warmth of the room and of her body, and we are okay.

We are okay.

chapter fourteen

THREE ORANGES. A bag of wheat bread. A note that reads, *Out Christmas shopping. Don't steal anything—I know where you live!* Two mugs in front of a full electric coffeepot.

"Power's back," I say, and Mabel nods.

She points to the note. "Funny guy."

"Yeah. But kind of sweet."

"Completely."

I don't think I've ever fallen asleep in a dark place and woken to see it in the light for the first time. Last night I made out the objects but the color was missing. Now I see the windows, that their frames are painted a forest green. If it weren't completely white outside, the shade of the paint would match the trees. The curtains are patterned with blue and yellow flowers.

"You think Tommy picked these out?" I ask.

"I hope he did," Mabel says. "But no, I don't think so."

"Do you think he killed that deer?"

She turns toward the mantel as though the deer could speak and tell her.

"No. Do you?"

"No," I say.

Mabel opens up the bag of bread and takes out four slices.

"I guess we can go back when we're ready," she says.

I pour us each a cup of coffee. I give her the better mug. I take the seat with the better view because I've always cared more about what I'm looking out at than she has.

The kitchen table's legs are uneven; every time we lean forward it tilts. We drink our coffees black because he has no cream and we eat our toast dry because we can't find butter or jam. And I look outside most of the time that we sit here, but sometimes I look at Mabel instead. The morning light on her face. The waves in her hair. The way she chews with her mouth the slightest bit open. The way she licks a crumb off her finger.

"What?" she asks, catching me smiling.

"Nothing," I say, and she smiles back.

I don't know if I still love her in the way that I used to, but I still find her just as beautiful.

She peels an orange, separates it in perfect halves, and gives one of them to me. If I could wear it like a friendship bracelet, I would. Instead I swallow it section by section and tell myself it means even more this way. To chew and to swallow in silence here with her. To taste the same thing in the same moment.

"I swear," Mabel says, "I feel like I could eat all day."

"I bought so much food. Do you think it went bad last night?"

"Doubtful. It's freezing."

Before long, we're washing our breakfast dishes and leaving them on a dish towel to dry. We're gathering up blankets from last night and setting them on the coffee table, folding the bed back in until it's only a couch again. We're standing in the empty space where the bed was, looking out the window at the snow.

"You think we'll make it back?" Mabel asks.

"I hope so."

We find a pen and write on the back of Tommy's note, include lots of thank-yous and exclamation points.

"Ready?" I ask her.

"Ready," she says.

But I don't think it's possible to prepare yourself for cold like this. It steals our breath. It chokes us.

"When we round that corner we'll see the dorm." That's all I can get out—each breath hurts.

Tommy cleared the small road earlier this morning, but it's slick and icy. We have to concentrate on each step. I watch my feet for so long. When I look up again the dorm is ahead of us in the distance, but to get there we have to step off the road Tommy cleared and into the perfect snow, and when we do we find how much has fallen. Snow is halfway up our calves, and we aren't wearing the right pants for that. It seeps through. It hurts. Mabel's shoes are thin leather boots, made for city streets in California. They'll be drenched by the time we make it to the door, probably ruined.

Maybe we should have waited for Tommy to return and drive us back, but we're out here now, so we keep going. I don't know that I've ever seen such a clear sky, blue and piercing, sharp in a way I didn't know the sky could be. Mabel's lips are purple; shivering doesn't begin to describe what my body's doing. Now we're close, though. The building towers above us, and I feel for the cold keys with fingers so stiff they can hardly bend to grasp them, and somehow I get the key into the lock but we can't pull open the door. We scoop snow off the ground with our hands, kick it away with our boots, pull at the door until it pushes the rest away in an arc, like one wing of a snow angel, and then we let it shut behind us.

"Shower," Mabel says in the elevator, and when we reach my floor I run into my room and grab the towels, and we step into separate shower stalls and pull off our clothing, too desperate for warmth to let the moment be awkward.

We stay under the water for so long. My legs and my hands are numb and then they're burning and then, after a long time, a familiar feeling returns to them.

Mabel finishes first; I hear her water shut off. I give her some time to go back to my room. I'm not sorry to stay under the hot water for a little while longer.

Mabel's right: The food is still cold. We're side by side in the rec room, peering into the refrigerator, heat pumping through the vents.

"You bought all of this?" she asks.

"Yes," I say, but I don't need to. My name is still on everything.

"I vote chili," she says.

"There's corn bread to go with it. And butter and honey."

"Oh my *God*, that sounds good."

We open and shut all the drawers and cabinets until we've found a pot for the chili, a grater for the cheese, a baking pan for the corn bread, and plates and silverware.

As I'm pouring the chili into the pot, Mabel says, "I have some news. *Good* news. I've been waiting for the right moment."

"Tell me."

"Carlos is having a baby."

"*What?*"

"Griselda's five months pregnant."

I shake my head in wonder. Her brother, Carlos, was away at college before the time Mabel and I became friends, so I've only met him a few times but . . . "You're going to be an aunt," I say.

"*Tía* Mabel," she says.

"Amazing."

"Right?"

"Yeah."

"They made us do this video conference call, my parents in the city, me at school, them in Uruguay—"

"Is that where they're living now?"

"Yeah, until Griselda finishes her doctorate. I was annoyed, it took forever to get the call to work, and then when they finally showed up on my screen all I saw was her little belly. I started bawling. My parents were both bawling. It was awesome. And it came at a perfect time, because they were all emotional about clearing Carlos's stuff out of his room. Not that they didn't *want* to. They were just, like, *Our son is all grown up and he'll never be our little boy again!* And then they were, like, *Grandchild!*"

"They'll be the best grandparents."

"They're already buying stuff for the baby. Everything is gender neutral because it's going to be a surprise."

I think of Mabel and her little niece or nephew. About her traveling to Uruguay to meet this new life. And watching a person grow, from inside a round belly, to a baby, to a kid who can tell her things. I think of Ana and Javier, so excited, remembering who they were when Carlos was young.

I almost gasp.

I don't know if I've ever thought this way about the expansiveness of a life. I think about it as it is in the wider world—in nature and time, in centuries and galaxies—but to think of Ana and Javier being young and in love, having their first baby, and watching him grow up, get married, move across the world. Knowing that they'll soon have another descendant to love. Knowing that they'll grow older as time passes, they'll become old the way Gramps was, with gray hair and a tremble in his step, so much love still in their hearts—this astonishes me. I am capsized.

Despite the sweetness of the news, loneliness, bottomless and black, rushes in.

I want to know what Gramps felt when he learned my mom was pregnant. She was young, and the boy wasn't in the picture, but surely, Gramps must have felt some gladness in spite of it. I wonder if, once the shock passed, he whooped and danced at the thought of me.

She tells me more about Carlos and Griselda's plans, what the due date is, what names she likes.

"I'm making lists," she says. "I'll read them to you. I mean, I'm sure they'll come up with their own but what if I find the perfect name?"

I'm trying to stay here with her in her happiness.

"I'd love to hear them," I say.

"Oh no!" she says, pointing.

The chili got too hot—it's bubbling and spilling over. We turn it down to a simmer. The corn bread still has twenty minutes to go.

I listen to her ideas about nurseries and what she'll do in lieu of a baby shower since she won't be able to travel that far during the spring semester. I last as long as I can, I do, I just can't shake the loneliness.

So when there's a break in the conversation, when it seems like the topic of her niece or nephew has passed, I sit at the table and she sits across from me.

"You said he was cute," I say. "Gramps was."

Her brow furrows. "I apologized for that."

"No," I say. "*I'm* sorry. Tell me again."

She looks at me.

"Please."

She shrugs.

"He was just . . . always doing these adorable things. Like polishing those candlesticks. Who does that?"

He would sit at the round table in the kitchen, humming along with the radio, shining the brass until it shone.

"And playing cards with his friends all day, like it was their job or something, saying it kept his mind sharp when really it was about drinking whiskey and having company, right? And winning money?"

I nodded. "He won more often than the others. I think that's how he sent me here. A couple decades of winning at small-stakes poker."

She smiles.

"All of those sweets he made. How he loved when I spoke Spanish, and the songs he sang, and the lectures he gave us. I wish we had listened better. I feel like there was so much more we could have learned from him." She shoots me a quick glance and says, "At least *I* could have learned so much more. I don't want to speak for you."

"No," I say. "I've thought of that, too. It was impossible to know what the subject of the lecture would be until he started it. And some of them felt so random at the time, but maybe they weren't. Once, he did a three-day series on stain removal."

"Like, for laundry?"

"Yeah, but with lots of variations. It went beyond clothes. How to get a stain out of a carpet, when to use fizzy water and when to use bleach, how to test to see if the colors would bleed."

"Amazing."

"Yeah, but I really learned it. I can get stains out of anything."

"I'll keep that in mind," she says. "Don't be surprised if you get packages of my laundry."

"What have I started?"

We smile; the joke settles.

"I miss his face," Mabel says.

"Me, too."

The deep lines by his eyes and mouth, in the center of his forehead. His short, coarse eyelashes and ocean-blue eyes. His nicotine-stained teeth and his wide grin.

"And how he loved jokes," she says, "but always laughed the hardest at his own."

"It's true."

"There are so many other things, too, that are harder to put into words. I could try, if you want me to."

"No," I say. "It's enough."

I stop my mind from taking me back to that last night and my discoveries. Instead, I play each thing that Mabel said over and picture them all, one by one, until they turn into other memories, too. How it sounded when he walked the hall in his plaid slippers, how clean and short he kept his fingernails, the low rattle of his throat clearing. A soft glow settles in, a whisper of what used to be. It fends off some of the loneliness.

And then I think of something else Mabel said.

"Why were they clearing out Carlos's room?"

She cocks her head.

"For you. I already told you they redid it."

"But I thought you meant the guest room."

"That room is tiny. And it's for *guests*."

"Oh," I say. A mechanical *ding* blares. "I guess I just assumed . . ."

The *ding* repeats. It's the oven timer. I'd almost forgotten where we were. I don't know what I'm trying to say anyway, so I check on our corn bread and find it risen and golden.

Something is shifting inside me. A heavy cloud passing. A glimpse of brightness. My name painted on a door.

After searching a row of drawers I discover a worn oven mitt, covered in illustrated gingerbread men. I show Mabel.

"How seasonally appropriate," she says.

"Right?"

It's so threadbare the pan's heat seeps through, but I manage to drop the loaf on the stovetop before it hurts too much. The scent fills the room.

We spoon chili into mismatched bowls from the cabinet and heap them with sour cream and pre-shredded cheese. We spoon out the honey for the corn bread, unwrap the butter.

"I want to hear about your life," I say. I know I should have told her this months ago. I should have told her yesterday and the day before that.

Mabel tells me about Los Angeles, about all of the name-dropping that goes on around her, about how lost she felt in her first few weeks there, but how lately she's been feeling more at home. We look up the website for Ana's gallery, and Mabel tells me about her most recent art show. I scroll through butterfly images, each wing made of fragments of photographs and then hand-dyed in rich pigments until the photographs are unrecognizable.

"I could tell you what they're about," she says. "But I'm sure you can figure it out on your own."

I ask her who she's heard from, and she tells me that Ben's liking Pitzer. She says he's been asking about me. He's been worried, too. They keep saying they'll get together one weekend, but that Southern California is huge. Going anywhere takes forever, and they're both settling into their own new routines anyway. "It feels good to know he's there, though. Not too far away if I needed a friend from home." She pauses. "You remember that there are other people in New York, too, right?"

I shake my head. I hadn't even thought about it for so long.

"Courtney's at NYU."

I laugh. "That's never going to happen."

"Eleanor's at Sarah Lawrence."

"I never really got to know her."

"Yeah, me neither, but she's really funny. How far is Sarah Lawrence from here?"

"What are you trying to do?"

"I just don't want you to be alone."

"And *Courtney* and *Eleanor* are somehow going to fix that?"

"Okay," she says. "You're right. I'm acting desperate."

I stand up to clear our dishes, but after I stack them, I just set them aside. I sit back down, swipe my hand across the table to sweep away the crumbs.

"I want to hear more," I say. "We got off track."

"I already told you about my favorite classes. . . ."

"Tell me about Jacob," I say.

She blinks, hard.

"We don't have to talk about him."

"It's okay," I say. "He's a part of your life. I want to hear about him."

"I don't even know how serious it is," she says, but I know that she's lying. The way she talks to him at night. The way she says *I love you.*

I look at her and wait.

"I can show you a picture," she says. I nod.

Out comes her phone. She swipes a few times and then decides on one. They're sitting next to each other at the beach, shoulders touching. He's wearing sunglasses and a baseball cap, so I'm not sure what I'm supposed to be seeing. I look at the image of her instead. Her wide smile, her hair in a braid over her shoulder, her bare arms, and the way she's leaning into him.

"You guys look happy together," I say. It comes out true and simple. It comes out without bitterness or regret.

"*Thanks,*" Mabel whispers.

She takes the phone back. She puts it in her pocket.

A minute passes. Maybe a few of them.

Mabel takes the plates I stacked to the sink. She washes them, both plates, both bowls, and the pot and the pan, and the silverware. At some point I get up and find a dish towel. She scrubs the splattered chili off the stove while I dry everything and put it away.

chapter fifteen

IT WAS A SUMMER OF STAYING OUT LATE, a summer of wandering. It was no longer a given that I'd be home for dinner, as though Gramps and I were practicing for our near futures without each other. Some nights early on he left food out for me. Once or twice I called to tell him I'd bring leftovers from something Javier made. Slowly, the dinners tapered off altogether. I feared he wasn't eating, but he wouldn't admit to it when I asked him. One day I went to the basement to do the laundry and found one of his socks was stuffed with bloody handkerchiefs. Seven of them. I laid them out one by one and used the tricks he taught me. I waited by the washer for its full cycle, hoping it would work. All seven came out clean, but my throat stayed tight, my stomach ached.

I folded them, one by one, in little squares. I carried

them upstairs on the top of the pile. Gramps was in the dining room when I got there, pouring himself a glass of whiskey.

He eyed the folded laundry.

"How've you been feeling, Gramps?"

He cleared his throat.

"So-so," he said.

"Have you been to the doctor?"

He snorted—my suggestion was ridiculous—and I remembered a time in junior high when I came home from health class and talked to him about the dangers of smoking.

"This conversation is very American," he'd said.

"We live in America."

"That we do, Sailor. That we do. But wherever in the world we live, something's gonna get us in the end. Something gets us every time."

I hadn't known then how to argue his point.

I should have tried harder.

"You never touch this stuff," he said now, holding up the bottle of whiskey. "Right?"

I shook my head.

"Besides that one time, I mean," he said.

"That was the only time."

"Good," he said. "Good." He twisted the top back onto the bottle and picked up his glass. "You have a couple minutes? I have some things to show you."

"Sure."

He gestured toward the dining table where some papers were spread out. He said, "Sit with me."

In front of me were documents from my soon-to-be college, thanking us for our payment in full for the first two semesters. There was an envelope with my social security card and my birth certificate. I didn't know he had them. "And this," he said, "is the information for your new bank account. It looks like a lot of money. It *is* a lot of money. But it will run out. After you're gone, no more four-dollar coffee. This is food and bus-fare money. Textbooks and simple clothing."

My heart pounded. My eyes burned. He was all I had.

"Here is your new ATM card. The code is four-oh-seven-three. Write that down somewhere."

"I can just use my normal card," I said. "From the account I share with you." I looked again at the dollar amount on the statement. It was more money than I had ever seen belong to us. "I don't need all this."

"You do," he said. Then he paused and cleared his throat. "You will."

"But all I care about is having you."

He leaned back in his chair. Took off his glasses. Cleaned them. Put them back on.

"Sailor."

His eyes were yellow as daisies. He'd been coughing up blood. He looked like a skeleton, sitting there next to me.

He shook his head and said, "You've always been a smart girl."

It was a summer of trying not to think too deeply. A summer of pretending that the end wasn't coming. A summer when I got lost in time, when I rarely knew what day it was, rarely cared about the hour. A summer so bright and warm it made me believe the heat would linger, that there would always be more days, that blood on handkerchiefs was an exercise in stain removal and not a sign of oblivion.

It was a summer of denial. Of learning what Mabel's body could do for mine, what mine could do for hers. A summer spent in her white bed, her hair fanned over the pillow. A summer spent on my red rug, sunshine on our faces. A summer when love was everything, and we didn't talk about college or geography, and we rode buses and hopped in cars and walked city blocks in our sandals.

Tourists descended onto our beach, sat in our usual places, so we borrowed Ana's car and crossed the Golden Gate to find a tiny piece of ocean to have for ourselves. We ate fish-and-chips in a dark pub that belonged in a different country, and we collected beach glass instead of shells, and we kissed in the redwoods, we kissed in the water, we kissed in movie theaters all over the city during matinees and late-night showings. We kissed in bookstores and record stores and dressing rooms. We kissed outside of the Lexington because we were too young to get in. We looked inside its doors at all the women there with short hair and long hair, lipstick and tattoos, tight dresses and tight jeans, button-ups and camisoles, and we pictured ourselves among them.

We didn't talk about Mabel's departure, which was to come half a month before mine. We didn't talk about the blood on the handkerchiefs or the coughs that ricocheted from the back of my house. I didn't tell her about the paperwork and the new ATM card, and I barely thought about them—only when I found myself without Mabel, only in the darkest and most silent hours—and when I did, I pushed the thoughts away.

But it turns out that even the fiercest denial can't stop time. And there we were, at her house. There, in her foyer, were the suitcases and duffel bags she'd packed when I wasn't looking. They'd be loading the car the next morning. Ana and Javier invited me to come on the round-trip drive to Los Angeles, but I couldn't bear the thought of returning without her, the only backseat passenger, and Mabel looked relieved when I said no.

"I think I would have cried the whole way," she told me in her room that night. "I might cry the whole way anyway, but if I'm alone you won't have to watch me do it."

I tried to smile but I failed. The trouble with denial is that when the truth comes, you aren't ready.

We opened her laptop. We looked for directions from

Los Angeles to Dutchess County. It was a forty-hour drive. We said forty hours didn't seem like that much; we'd expected it to be longer. We could meet in Nebraska and then it would only be twenty hours for each of us. *No problem*, we said, but we couldn't meet each other's eyes.

It was the middle of the night when Mabel whispered, "We aren't going to meet in Nebraska, are we?"

I shook my head. "We don't even have cars."

"There are the breaks," she said. "We'll both come home for those."

"Everyone says four years, but really it's just a few months at a time, and then a few months home every summer."

She nodded. She ran her hand along the side of my face.

And the morning came too soon. So much brightness, so much clatter in the kitchen. I knew I wouldn't be able to stomach anything, so I put on my clothes and I left before breakfast. I listened to the same heartbroken song the entire bus ride home, because it was still a summer when sadness was beautiful.

chapter sixteen

OUR TIME IS RUNNING OUT, and I'm not ready. I'm feeling the dorm's emptiness again. It's settling in, that it's not going to transform for Christmas, that it's going to look exactly the same as it does now, only one person emptier. It won't be warmer inside or blink with lights or smell like pine. It won't fill with Gramps's songs. Where did our ornaments go? The little angel bell. The painted horse, the tiny tree, the letter *M* stitched with sequins.

It's noon, and then it's one. I keep looking at my phone because I don't want the time to sneak up on me.

It's two, and my body is heavy and sinking, and I can't shake the feeling that everything is ending all over again; only it's worse this time because I know what awaits me when it's over.

It's two thirty.

There's still so much I need to tell her.

She hasn't asked me anything else about Gramps. She hasn't mentioned the name Birdie since last night. I know that feeling—of not wanting to know—but at the same time I think that she would listen if I started. I think we're playing a game without meaning to. We both want the other one of us to go first.

It's three before I say anything, but then I have to start. I force myself to start.

"I need to tell you what happened after you left," I say.

We are back in my room, sitting on the rug, looking through a stack of Hannah's magazines. I see pages of perfect houses and perfect outfits but I can't concentrate on any of the words that accompany them.

Mabel closes her magazine and sets it down. She looks at me.

chapter seventeen
AUGUST

THE MORNINGS AFTER SHE LEFT, I woke up early. I don't know why. I wanted to sleep the days away, but I couldn't. The fog was heavy over the rooftops and telephone wires and trees, and I would make myself tea and then go back to my room to read and wait until the sun broke through.

Then I would go to Ocean Beach.

I'd sit by myself in the spot where Mabel and I used to hang out and stare out at the water. I was trying to remember my mother. I didn't think of it that way for all those years I'd been doing it, but it was clear to me by then. The waves would come in, and I would try to remember the way she must have looked up on her surfboard, how she would have dragged it behind her as she came back to shore, how she would have waved to me with her other hand. Maybe I sat right here with her friends. Maybe the buried memories of those days are what led me back each time.

It was mid-August, and Mabel had left just a few days before, and I was supposed to leave in a little over two weeks. That morning was quiet, only a couple of guys surfing in the distance. When they got out of the water they stood around talking, and at one point I saw them look over at me. I could feel what they were saying. Two of them were telling a third who I was.

It felt so unfair, that they could remember her and I couldn't. Maybe if I closed my eyes, just listened. I knew that smells triggered memories, so I breathed in deep. And then I heard a voice. It was one of the guys. The other two were gone.

"Marin," he said. "Right?"

"Yes."

I squinted up at him, wondered if my hair reminded him of hers. I thought he might tell me about something intangible. An aura I gave off or a gesture I made.

"What are you waiting around for?"

"Nothing," I said.

But it wasn't true. I was waiting for a faraway nostalgia to take him over, the way it always did with all the others. I almost held out my hand, sure he'd drop shells in. Maybe the feeling of them in my palm would do it.

"I heard you looked a lot like your mom, but this is ridiculous."

He didn't sound dreamy at all, but I smiled anyway and said thanks.

"I've got a van in the lot and some time to spare," he said.

My body tensed. In spite of the lead in my stomach, in spite of the way I was sinking into the sand, darkness rushing in, I made my voice stronger. "Who *are* you even?" I asked.

"I'm Fred," he said.

"Never even heard of you."

I turned to the ocean and watched the waves crash. The more focused I was on them, the louder they were, the closer they became. When a wave reached the toe of my shoe, I stood up.

I was alone, just like I'd hoped, but it felt terrible.

I needed something.

Ana, I thought, but that was stupid. Ana was not mine.

I needed a warm place, music, sweet-smelling rooms.

Traffic parted for me; the darkening sky held its light until I unlocked my door and rushed upstairs.

"Gramps," I called. "Emergency! I need cake!"

He wasn't in the living room or the dining room. The kitchen was empty, nothing on the stove or in the oven.

"Gramps?"

I stood still and listened. Quiet. He must have been out, I thought, but I found myself at the door of his study. I saw him. Couldn't believe it but there he was at his desk. Cigarette smoldering in the crystal ashtray, pen in hand, staring blankly off.

"Gramps?"

"Not a good time."

His voice wasn't even his voice.

"Sorry," I said, backing away.

I found my way to the love seat. I wanted a lecture about anything. The correct name for a coffee establishment. The duplicity of nuns. The difference between carnal desire and the love for someone's soul.

I wanted to touch knees under the table.

I wanted him to tell me about my mother.

Night fell and he didn't come out. He didn't make dinner. I sat on the love seat, perfectly still, until my back got sore and my feet fell asleep and I had to stand to get the blood rushing again. I got ready for bed and then I went to my room in the front of the house, where nobody ever went but me.

chapter eighteen

"MARIN," she says. "Please talk to me."

I guess I've gone silent. I didn't even realize it.

"*I miss him,*" I whisper. It isn't what I expected to say; it just comes out. I don't even know if it's true. I do miss him, but then I don't.

She scoots closer.

"I know," she says. "I know. But you're trying to tell me something. I want to hear it."

Her knee is so close to mine. She isn't afraid to touch me now that we've held each other all night. I love her, but there is no going back. No bonfires on the beach. No mouths pressed together. No hungry fumblings. No fingers through her hair. But maybe I can go further back, to a less complicated time when *cute* was an accurate description of my grandfather and Mabel was simply my best friend.

I want to tell her, but I can't do it yet. The words are stuck.

"Tell me something," I say.

"What?"

"Anything."

Tell me about heat.

Tell me about the beach.

Tell me about a girl who lives in a house with her grandfather, about a house that's full of easy love, about a house that isn't haunted. Hands covered in cake flour and air that smells sweet. Tell me about the way the girl and her grandfather did each other's laundry and left it folded in the living room, not because there were secrets, but because that's just the way they were: simple and easy and true.

But before she can say anything, the words come.

"None of it was real," I tell her.

She scoots closer, our thighs touch. She takes my hands in hers like we used to do on the beach, like I'm freezing and she can warm me.

"None of what was real?"

"*Him*," I whisper.

"I don't understand," she says.

"He had a walk-in closet behind his room. It's where he really lived. It was filled with all this *stuff*."

"What kind of stuff?"

"Letters, to start. They were all written by him. He signed her name, but he wrote all of them."

"Marin, I don't . . ."

chapter nineteen

GRAMPS'S LEAVING WOKE ME UP. The door shutting, footsteps down the stairs. I peered out to the street and saw him turn the corner in the direction of the store, or Bo's house, or any number of the places he disappeared to during his walks through the neighborhood.

I'd slept in. It was already eleven when I got into the shower. Once out, I boiled some eggs and left two in a bowl for him. I made tea for myself and then placed a second bag into a teacup for him to find when he returned. I read on the sofa for a while. Then I went out. I spent the rest of the day in Dolores Park with Ben and Laney, throwing the ball for her, laughing with Ben, going over every shared memory from the last seven years of our lives. We tied Laney to a pole outside Ben's favorite taqueria and watched all the hipsters stop and pet her.

"How will you live without this?" he said as we bit into our burritos. "*Is* there even Mexican food in New York?"

"Honestly? I have no idea."

It was past eight when I got home, and immediately, I felt the stillness.

"Gramps?" I called, but just like the night before, he didn't answer.

His door was closed. I knocked and waited. Nothing. The car was out front. I took the stairs to the basement in case he was doing laundry, but the machines were silent.

In the kitchen, the eggs I'd left him were untouched in their bowl, the tea bag dry in the cup.

Ocean Beach. I would look for him there. I grabbed a sweater and went out to the street. The sky was darkening and the headlights on the Great Highway shone as I darted across. I ran onto the sand and up through the dunes. Beach grass grazed my ankles, a flock of birds flew overhead, and then I was passing the warning sign that everybody ignored, even though the danger it warned of was undeniably true. I thought of Gramps's soaking pants legs, of his skeleton body, of the blood on the handkerchiefs. I had a clear view of the water now, but not enough light to make out details. I wished for my mother's friends, but skilled as they were, even they didn't surf at dusk.

There were a few clusters of people out walking, a couple lone figures with dogs. No old men that I could see. I turned back.

Inside again, I knocked on his door.

Silence.

Panic tilted my vision.

A succession of flights and drops. The right throbs and the wrong.

This was my mind, playing tricks on me. I was being hysterical. Gramps left the house all the time, and I had barely been home all summer, so why would he be here now, for me? I stood right on the other side of his door. *"Gramps!"* I screamed. It was so loud he couldn't have slept through it, and when silence still followed, I told myself that everything was fine.

In the kitchen, I put a pot of water on the stove. *Before the water reaches a boil, he will be here.* I dropped the pasta in and set the timer. *Before the ten minutes are up.* I melted some butter. I wasn't hungry, but I would eat it anyway, and by the time I was done, he would walk through the door and call out my name.

The clock ticked. I ate as slowly as I could. But then the bowl was empty, and I was still alone. I didn't know what was happening. I was trying to understand. I was crying, trying not to cry.

I picked up the phone and dialed Jones's house. I made my voice steady. "Nope," Jones said. "Saw him yesterday. I'll be seeing him tomorrow." I called Bo. "Poker's *tomorrow* night," he told me. I went back to his door. I banged so hard

I could have knocked it down, but there was that knob, and I knew all I had to do was turn it.

Instead I picked up my phone again. Javier answered.

"You've looked everywhere?" he asked me.

"Not in his room. His door is closed."

I heard the confusion in Javier's pause.

"Open it, Marin," he finally said. "Go ahead and open it."

"But what if he's in there?" My voice was so small.

"It will be slow crossing Market, but we'll be there as soon as we can."

"I'm alone," I said. I didn't even know what I was saying.

"I am calling the police. They'll probably be there before we will. You just wait. We are coming to you. We can do it together. We're leaving now."

I didn't want him to hang up, but he did, and my hands were shaking and I was facing the closed door. I turned away from it, toward the picture of my mother. I needed her. I took it off the wall. I needed to see it better. I would take it out of its glass frame. Maybe holding it in my hands would help me remember. Maybe I would feel her with me.

At the coffee table, I knelt on the carpet and lifted the small metal tabs that held the frame back in place. I lifted the cardboard, and there was the yellowed back of the photograph, with a line in Gramps's handwriting: *Birdie on Ocean Beach, 1996.* My vision doubled, then righted itself. The dark pressed against me.

Maybe my mind was taking me in convoluted directions. Maybe Birdie was just like *sweetheart* or *honey*, a name that could apply to anyone.

I opened his doors for the first time.

Here I was, in his study. In the fifteen years I'd lived there, I'd never stepped inside. One wall was lined with shelves and on the shelves were boxes and boxes of letters. Hands shaking, I reached for one. The envelope was addressed to his PO box. The handwriting was his own.

I unfolded the paper.

Daddy, it said. *The mountains look beautiful today. When are you going to visit me? Just for a little while? Marin has school and her own friends. You can leave her for a couple weeks.* I stopped reading. I turned to the letter behind it. Addressed to Claire Delaney, Colorado, no stamp, never sent. I pulled out the paper. *You know I can't do that. Not yet. But soon. Soon.* I grabbed another box of letters. They were all from him to her, or from her to him. They were all in his handwriting. They dated back so many years. I was trying to read, but my vision kept blurring.

I heard faraway sirens. I left his study and walked into his bedroom.

It smelled like cigarettes and tea. It smelled like him. His bed was made and everything was tidy. It struck me for the first time, how wrong it was that I'd never seen it. How wrong to have been shut out. The door to his closet was open, all of his sweaters folded with precision. I opened a dresser drawer to the shirts I'd washed and folded for him a couple days before. I opened a smaller drawer and saw his stacks of handkerchiefs. I knew I was looking for something, but I didn't know what.

The sirens were getting louder. And then I saw it. A worn velvet armchair, sitting against a door.

I pushed the chair away.

I turned the knob.

It was a small space, somewhere between a room and a closet, and it was dark until I saw the chain dangling from the ceiling and pulled it, and light shone across all of my mother's things. They were preserved as if for a museum in clear bags with cedar blocks, labeled SHIRTS, PANTS AND SHORTS, UNDERGARMENTS AND SWIMWEAR, DRESSES, SHOES. SCHOOL PAPERS, NOTES AND LETTERS, POSTERS AND SOUVENIRS, BOOKS AND MAGAZINES. Photographs of her covered the expanse of one wall. Every square inch, all these images he never showed me. She was a little girl in ruffles, a teenager in ripped jeans, a young woman in bathing suits and wet suits, a young mother holding a baby—holding *me*.

The sirens stopped. There was a pounding at the door.

"*Police!*" they yelled.

In every picture, my mother was a stranger. I didn't know where Gramps was, but I knew I could never see him again. Never.

There must have been a crash as the front door burst open.

There must have been footsteps, coming toward me.

They must have been calling for anyone who was home.

But nobody hurried me as I took it all in. Nobody said anything as I turned back to the clothing, took the bag marked DRESSES, and unzipped it, just to be sure, and found the deep green fabric. It unfurled like it did that day he held it up for me and didn't let me touch it.

I let it drop to the floor. I turned around.

Two police officers stood watching me.

"Are you Marin Delaney?"

I nodded.

"We got a call saying you needed help."

My body was heavy with longing, my heart—for the first time—full of hate.

They were waiting for me to say something.

"Take me away from here," I said.

"We'll go over to the station," one of the cops told me.

"Sure you don't want to grab a sweater?" the other one asked.

I shook my head.

"Sorry about this," he said as I climbed into the backseat behind a metal grate. "It's a quick ride."

They sat me in a chair in an office. They brought me a

glass of water and then another. They left me alone and then came back.

"Was he acting erratic?" one of them asked.

I didn't know. He was acting like Gramps.

They waited.

"What does it mean to act erratic?"

"I'm sorry, honey. Do you need a minute? We just need all the information on record."

"Let's just move on to the next question," the other one said. "Do you know if your grandfather has a history of mental illness?"

I laughed. "You saw that room."

"Any other indications?"

"He thought his friends were poisoning his whiskey," I said. "So there's that."

I couldn't bring myself to talk about the letters. They were there if they wanted to see them.

"What makes you believe that your grandfather may be missing?"

What did it mean, to be missing? What did it mean, to believe? All I knew was green fabric, unfurling. Eggs, untouched. Secret rooms and photographs. Tea and coffee and cigarettes. A made bed. A pair of slippers. Silence. The thousands of secrets he kept from me.

"I think he had cancer," I said. "There was blood on the handkerchiefs."

"Cancer," one of them said, and wrote it down.

I looked at his notepad. Everything I told them was there, as though my answers really meant something, as though they would reveal the truth.

"Blood on handkerchiefs," I said. "Will you write that, too?"

"Sure, honey," he said, and wrote the words down neatly.

"We have a couple witnesses who saw an old man going into the water at Ocean Beach," the other said, and I already knew it, I guess. How easily the ocean must have swept him away. I already knew it but I felt my body go rigid, as though I were the dead one. "We have a search team out there now trying to find him. But if he's the one they saw, he's been missing for more than eight hours."

"*Eight* hours? What time is it?"

The office's only window was into the hallway. Outside, it must have been daylight.

"There are a couple people in the lobby waiting for you. Mr. and Mrs. Valenzuela."

I thought of Gramps being swallowed by the water. It would have been so cold. No wet suit. Just his thin T-shirt, his bare arms. His thin skin, all his scratches and bruises.

"I'm really tired," I said.

"I'm sure they could drive you home."

I never wanted to see him again. I never would. And yet—how would I step foot inside our house without him? The loss snuck up on me, black and cavernous.

I thought of Ana and Javier, and how kindly they would look at me, and the things they might say, and how I would have to tell them what I'd discovered and how I knew that I couldn't.

My voice was thick. "I think I'll take a cab."

"They seem concerned about you. They've been waiting for a long time."

He must have been freezing.

I thought of his tears.

"We'll get a cab for you, honey. If you're sure that's what you want."

chapter twenty

"I'M HAVING TROUBLE UNDERSTANDING," Mabel says. "Birdie was your mother?"

"Birdie was my mother. And all of the things that she sent him were things he already owned. And all of the letters she wrote him were things he wrote to himself. *You write a letter, you get a letter.*"

"Wouldn't you have known if it was his handwriting?"

"I never saw the envelopes," I say. "I didn't even have a key to the mailbox."

"Okay," Mabel says. "Okay."

"He had all of it. He had pictures of me and pictures of her. He had a fucking museum back there and he never showed me any of it. I could have *known* her. None of what we had was real. *He* wasn't real."

She's forgotten to rub my hands; she's just squeezing them.

"But it was just grief, right? He *was* real. He was just, I don't know, brokenhearted."

Was he? I thought he never lied to me. I thought I knew who he was, but he was a stranger all along, and how do I mourn a stranger? And if the person I loved wasn't even a person, then how can he be dead? This is what happens when I let myself think too much. I squeeze shut my eyes. I want darkness, stillness, but light cuts in.

"*Is he dead?*" I ask her. My voice is a whisper, the smallest version of itself. This is the thing I'm most afraid to say. The craziest thing, the thing that makes me too much like him. "I don't know if he's dead."

"Hey," she says. "Look at me."

"They said he drowned. But they didn't find him. They never found him. Do bodies disappear that way? Really?"

"Look at me," Mabel says, but I can't. "Look at me," she says again.

I'm looking at the seams of my jeans. I'm looking at the threads in the rug. I'm looking at my shaking hands that I've snatched back from hers, and I'm sure I must be losing my mind. Like Gramps, like poor Mr. Rochester's locked-up wife, like the howling woman in the motel room next to mine.

"Marin, he died," Mabel says. "Everyone knows that. We knew he was lost in the ocean. It was in the newspaper. We just didn't know how it happened."

"But how do we really know?"

"We just do," she says. "We just know."

We just know. We just know.

"But does it really happen like that?"

"Yes," she says.

"But waves," I say. "The tide," I say.

"Yes. And currents that pull things under and send them far out. And rocks to get snagged on, and predators."

"But are you sure?"

"I'm sure."

"Those people who thought they saw him, they could have seen someone else."

She doesn't answer me.

"It was dark," I say.

She's quiet.

"Marin," she says.

"It was really dark. You know how dark it is out there."

chapter twenty-one

AUGUST

YOU GO THROUGH LIFE thinking there's so much you need. Your favorite jeans and sweater. The jacket with the faux-fur lining to keep you warm. Your phone and your music and your favorite books. Mascara. Irish Breakfast tea and cappuccinos from Trouble Coffee. You need your yearbooks, every stiffly posed school-dance photo, the notes your friends slipped into your locker. You need the camera you got for your sixteenth birthday and the flowers you dried. You need your notebooks full of the things you learned and don't want to forget. You need your bedspread, white with black diamonds. You need your pillow—it fits the way you sleep. You need magazines promising self-improvement. You need your running shoes and your sandals and your boots. Your grade report from the semester you got straight As. Your prom dress, your shiny earrings, your pendants on delicate chains. You need your underwear, your light-colored bras and your black ones. The watercolor sunset hanging over your bed. The dozens and dozens of shells in glass jars.

The cab was waiting outside the station.

The airport, I said, but no sound came out.

"The airport," I said, and we pulled away.

You think you need all of it.

Until you leave with only your phone, your wallet, and a picture of your mother.

chapter twenty-two

AUGUST

I BARELY REMEMBER getting there. I walked up to the ticket counter and said I had a reservation.

"Do you have a flight number?"

I shook my head.

"Spell your name for me?"

I couldn't think of a single letter. I wiped my palms on my jeans.

At the station, the officers said, "You sure you don't know where he is?"

"I was in bed when he left."

"Miss? Will you spell it?"

"I'm sorry," I said. "I can't spell my name."

"I'm sorry," I told them. "I made him eggs but he didn't eat them."

"I found a reservation for Marin Delaney. SFO to LGA. But it's for the twenty-third."

"I'm early," I said.

"I can see that you're upset," they said.

"Let me see if I can get you on a flight today," she said. "There will be a fee."

I took out the ATM card.

The heat—it swallowed me up when I arrived in New York. All my life, hot days came with cooler breezes, but even with the sun setting, the air was thick and relentless.

I boarded a bus from the airport. I didn't know which direction I was going in, but it didn't really matter. I watched out the window until I saw a motel sign lighting up the dark. HOME AWAY FROM HOME, it said. I rang the bell to get off at the next stop. The moment I stepped into the lobby, I knew it was no place to be. I should have left, but I crossed the room anyway.

"You over eighteen?" the man behind the counter asked me.

"Yes," I said.

He looked at me. "I'm gonna need ID."

I handed him my driver's license.

"How long you staying?"

"I'll check out on the twenty-third."

He ran my card, nodded, handed me a key.

I climbed the stairs and walked down a corridor to find room 217. I startled at the room before mine—a man stood in its window, staring.

I turned the key and stepped in.

Worse than stale. Worse than unclean.

I tried to open the windows to get the smell out, but they only opened three inches, and the air outside was still thick and hot. The curtains were stiff, coated in something. The carpet was splotchy and worn, the comforter torn. I put my photograph in its folder down on the chair along with my wallet and my phone.

Next door to me, a woman started howling and didn't stop. Below me, someone blasted telenovelas. I heard something break. It's possible that some of the rooms were occupied by regular people, down on their luck, but my wing was full of the broken, and I was at home among them.

By then it was late and I hadn't eaten anything. I was amazed that I could be hungry, but my stomach was churning and growling, so I crossed the street to the diner. I sat myself, like the sign told me to. I ordered a grilled cheese and french fries and a chocolate shake. I feared nothing would fill me up.

It was pitch-black when I headed back across the street. I asked the motel clerk for a toothbrush. She told me there was a drugstore across the street, but then handed me a travel kit that someone had left behind, still enclosed in plastic, with a tiny toothbrush and a tiny tube of paste. I walked past my neighbor, still staring out the window. As I splashed water on my face, I thought I heard Gramps singing, but when I turned the faucet off there was nothing.

I went back outside. I knocked on the door next to mine. The man opened it.

He had sunken cheeks and bloodshot eyes. He was the kind of person I'd cross the street to steer clear of.

"I need to ask you something," I said. "If you see an old man outside my room, will you knock on the wall to let me know?"

"Sure," he said.

And then I fell asleep, knowing he was watching.

Three nights later I heard a tap above my head. Would he be bloodstained, would he be ghostly? Outside it was quiet. There was no one. My neighbor's vacant eyes peered through the screen. I knew that he hadn't moved for a long time. It wasn't he who had knocked. Maybe a rodent, burrowing through walls. Maybe my mind, playing tricks. Maybe someone upstairs. Maybe him, haunting me.

He sang each time I turned on the faucet, so I stopped using the water.

There were only six days left before I could move into the dorms. At the drugstore, I bought a gallon of water for drinking and toothbrushing. I bought a bottle of hand sanitizer. I bought a pack of white T-shirts and a pack of white underwear. I bought baby powder for the oil in my hair.

I ordered split pea soup.

Scrambled eggs.

Coffee.

I used the ATM card.

I tipped eighteen percent.

I said thank you.

They said, "See you tonight."

"See you in the morning."

"The cherry pie is special today."

I said thank you.

I said see you.

I looked both ways.

I crossed the street.

I turned on the television. *Judge Judy*. Laugh tracks. Always. Dove. Swiffer.

I pulled back the blankets, ignored the stains. I burrowed under like a rodent in a wall. I kept trying to find the right position. I made myself very still. I made my eyes shut.

"You're okay," I told myself.

"Shhh," I said.

chapter twenty-three

"COME WITH ME," Mabel says.

Our talk is over. We're on the floor across from each other, each of us leaning against a bed. I should feel a weight lifted now that I've told her everything, but I don't. Not yet. Maybe in the morning some new feeling will settle.

"I promise, this is the last time I'll ask. Just come home for a few days."

If it weren't for the lies he told me.

If Birdie had been an elderly woman with beautiful penmanship.

If his coats were all that hung in the closet and he'd known his lungs were black and he drank his whiskey without suspicion.

If I could stop dreaming up a deathbed scene where his hospital blankets are crisp over his stomach and his hands are holding mine. Where he says something like, *See you on the other side, Sailor.* Or, *I love you, sweetheart.* And a nurse touches my shoulder and tells me it's over even though I can already see it by the peaceful stillness of him. *Take your time*, she says, so we just stay there, he and I, until the darkness falls and I am strong enough to leave the room without him.

"How am I supposed to leave you here?" Mabel asks.

"I'm sorry. I *will* go with you. Someday. But I can't do it tomorrow."

She picks at the frayed edges of the rug.

"Mabel."

She won't look at me.

Everything is quiet. I'd suggest going somewhere, just out for a walk even, but we're both confounded by the cold. The moon is framed perfectly in the window, a crescent of white against black, and I can see by its clearness that it isn't snowing anymore.

"I shouldn't have only called and texted. I should have flown to you."

"It's okay."

"He seemed sick for so long. Kind of frail or something."

"I know."

Her eyes tear over, and she looks out the window.

I wonder if she sees what I do. If she feels the same stillness.

Mabel, I want to say. *We don't have much time left.*
Mabel.

There is me and there is you and the snow has finished falling. Let's just sit here.

Sometime later, we stand side by side at the sinks in the bathroom. We look tired and something else, too. It takes me a minute to identify it. And then I know.

We look young.

Mabel smears toothpaste onto her toothbrush. She hands me the tube.

She doesn't say *Here you go.* I don't say *Thank you.*

I brush in the circular way you're supposed to. Mabel brushes back and forth, hard. I watch my reflection and concentrate on giving each tooth enough time.

Standing like this in Mabel's bathroom back home, we would never have been silent. There were always millions of things to talk about, each topic pressing in so that our conversations rarely began and ended but rather began and were interrupted and continued, strands of thoughts that got pushed aside and picked up later.

If our past selves got a glimpse of us now, what would they make of us?

Our bodies are the same but there's a heaviness in Mabel's shoulders, a weariness in the way my hip leans against the counter. A puffiness around her eyes, a darkness under mine. But more than those things, there's the separateness of us.

I didn't return Mabel's nine hundred texts because I knew we'd end up like this no matter what. What happened had broken us even if it wasn't about us at all. Because I know that for all her care and understanding, when this visit is over and she's back in LA with Jacob and her new friends, sitting in her lecture halls or riding the Ferris wheel in Santa Monica or eating dinner by herself in front of an open textbook, she'll be the same as she's always been—fearless and funny and whole. She'll still be herself and I'll be learning who I am now.

She spits into the sink. I spit into the sink. We rinse our brushes, *tap-tap*, in close succession.

Both faucets run as we splash our faces.

I don't know what she's thinking about. I can't even guess.

We walk back down the hallway, shut off the lights, and climb into opposite twin beds.

My eyes are open in the dark.

"Good night," I say.

She's quiet.

"I hope you don't think," she says, "that because of Jacob..." She looks at me for an indication that I understand.

She gives up. "It's not that I met him and forgot about you. I was trying to move on. You didn't give me other options. The night before I was supposed to go out with him I tried sending you another text. *Remember Nebraska?* That's what I wrote. I stayed up late hoping you'd answer me. I slept with the phone by my pillow. All it would have taken was one word from you and I wouldn't have gone. I would have waited longer, but you shut me out," she says. "I'm not trying to make you feel guilty. I understand now. Really. But I just need you to know how it happened. I'm happy now, with him, but I wouldn't be with him if you'd have answered me."

The pain when she says this, it's not her fault. Deep in my chest is still an aching hollowness, vacancy, fear. I can't imagine opening myself up to the rush of kissing her, can't imagine her hands under my clothes.

"I'm sorry," I say. "I know I'm the one who disappeared."

I can still see the moon out the window. I can still feel the stillness of the night. I can hear Mabel saying that Gramps is dead—*gone*—sounding so certain and I try to feel that certainty, too.

I try not to think of her heartbreak, how I caused it, but I can't keep it out and it rushes over me.

"I'm sorry," I say again.

"I know," Mabel says. "I understand."

"Thank you for coming," I say.

The hours stretch on, and I fall in and out of sleep, and at some point she slips out of bed and out of the room. She stays away for a long time, and I try to stay awake until she comes back, but I just wait and wait and wait.

When I wake up again at the first light of the morning, she's back in Hannah's bed, sleeping with her arm covering her eyes as if she could stave off the day.

chapter twenty-four

WHEN I OPEN MY EYES AGAIN, she isn't here. I'm seized with panic that I've missed her altogether, that she's already gone and I haven't gotten to say good-bye.

But here is her duffel open in the middle of my floor.

The thought of her slinging it over her shoulder and walking out is enough to make me double over. I have to fill the minutes between now and then with as much as I can.

I climb out of bed and take out the gifts I bought. I wish I had wrapping paper or at least some ribbon, but the tissue paper will have to do. I put on a bra and change into jeans and a T-shirt. I brush my hair. For some reason I don't want to be in my pajamas when I walk her down the stairs.

"Hey," she says from the doorway.

"Good morning," I say, trying not to cry. "I'll be right back."

I rush through peeing and brushing my teeth so that I can be back there, with her. I catch her before she zips up her suitcase.

"I was thinking we could wrap this in your clothes," I say, and hand her the vase I bought for her parents. She takes it from me and nestles it into her things. She goes to reach for the zipper but I stop her.

"Close your eyes and hold out your hands," I say.

"Shouldn't I wait?" she asks.

"Lots of people exchange gifts on Christmas Eve."

"But the thing I got you is—"

"I know. It doesn't matter. I want to see you open it."

She nods.

"Close your eyes," I say again.

She closes them. I look at her. I wish her everything good. A friendly cab driver and short lines through security. A flight with no turbulence and an empty seat next to her. A beautiful Christmas. I wish her more happiness than can fit in a person. I wish her the kind of happiness that spills over.

I place the bell into her open palms.

She opens her eyes and unwraps it.

"You noticed," she says.

"Ring it."

She does, and the tone lingers and we wait quietly until it's over.

"Thank you," she says. "It's so pretty."

She slings her bag over her shoulder, and it hurts just as much as I expected it to. I follow her into the elevator. When we get to the door, the cab is waiting in a sea of white.

"You're sure, right?" she asks.

"Yeah," I say.

She looks out the window.

She bites a nail.

"You're sure you're sure?"

I nod.

She takes a deep breath, manages a smile.

"Okay. Well. I'll see you soon."

She steps toward me and hugs me tight. I close my eyes. There will come a time soon—any second—when she'll pull away and this will be over. In my mind, we keep ending, ending. I try to stay here, now, for as long as we can.

I don't care that her sweater is scratchy. I don't care that the cab driver is waiting. I feel her rib cage expand and retract. We stay and stay.

Until she lets me go.

"See you soon," I say, but the words come out thick with despair.

I'm making the wrong choice.

The glass door opens. Cold rushes in.

She steps outside and shuts the door behind her.

When I lived with Jones and Agnes, it was their daughter, Samantha, who made me breakfast. Wheat bread and applesauce, every morning. We ate matching meals, perched on the stools in their kitchen. She'd look over my homework if I had questions, but I remember not wanting to ask for much help. She'd always scrunch up her forehead and say how it had been a long time since she learned this stuff. She'd figure it out eventually and talk me through it, but it was more fun to ask about her magazines because she delighted in talking about them. I learned what DUIs were because Paris Hilton and Nicole Richie both got them. The news of Tom Cruise and Katie Holmes's wedding was everywhere. I learned what to wait for with each new issue's release.

I rarely saw Jones and Agnes until after school, because they slept late and entrusted Samantha with my morning care. She was always nice to me after that. She always did my nails for free.

I don't have her number anymore. It's been a long time since she's lived with her parents. I wish I had it now. I call the salon, just in case she's there early doing work before it opens, but the phone rings and rings and then goes to voice mail. I listen to her voice slowly stating the hours and location.

I pace the room for a while, waiting for it to be ten in San Francisco. As soon as it's one here, I press call.

"It's you," Jones says when I say hello.

"Yeah," I say. "It's me."

"Where are you?"

"School."

He's quiet.

"I see," he says. "You spending the holiday with some fellow troublemakers?"

He's probably running inventory of who I could be with, envisioning a few of us here, a scrappy team of orphans and outcasts.

"Something like that," I say.

I should have prepared something to say to him. The truth is, I only called so that I could remind him—and myself, maybe—that I'm still a part of the world. It feels like now or never with him, and I'm not sure if I want to lose what's left of the life Gramps and I shared. I used to be sure, but now I'm not.

I'm about to ask how Agnes is, but he speaks before I get the words out.

"I have everything," he says. "Just so you know. Whether you want it or not, everything is here in the garage waiting for you. Not the beds or the refrigerator or nothin' like that. But the real stuff. The owner arranged an estate sale after the place was vacant thirty days. But the guys and I, we bought it all."

I close my eyes: brass candlesticks; the blue-and-gold blanket; my grandmother's china with the tiny red flowers.

"We all feel real bad about it," he says. "Feel like we shoulda done something. For you."

"What about the letters?"

Quiet.

He clears his throat.

"They're here. The landlord gave us the, uh, more *personal* stuff."

"Can you get rid of them?"

"I can do that."

"Keep the photographs, though. Okay?"

"Mm-hm," he says.

I think of all of those pictures that Gramps kept for himself. My jaw clenches with the wrongness of it. He should have sat next to me and shown me. He should have said, *Now, I think this was the time that . . .* or *Oh yes, I remember this day . . .* He should have told me all the ways in which I reminded him of her. He should have helped me remember her. He never should have let me forget.

Jones is still quiet. I hear his throat clearing.

"Your gramps, he was in a hospital a long time ago, when you stayed with us. Not sure if you remember. It almost killed him, so we didn't want to send him back there. Wish I could say that was the right decision. Wish I could say I didn't realize it got so bad again. *Wish* I could say that."

I breathe in and out. It requires effort. "I thought he was sick."

"Well, he was. Just in more ways than you thought."

He clears his throat again. I wait.

"Sometimes it's difficult," he says, "to know the right thing to do."

I nod even though he can't see me. There's no arguing with a statement like that, even if a different future is unfurling in my head—one where I knew what Gramps's prescriptions were for, and I watched to make sure he took them, and he took me along to his appointments and his doctors told me what to watch for.

I need to find something kind to say, something instead of these thoughts of how Gramps failed me, how Jones failed us. He knows it already; I can hear it in his voice.

"Merry Christmas Eve, Jones," I finally say, wanting the conversation to end.

"You get religious all of a sudden? If your gramps had a grave, he'd be turning in it."

It's a rough joke, the kind they used to make in my kitchen.

"It's just something to say," I tell him. Out the window, the snow is starting again. Not stormlike, just scattered flakes drifting. "Give Agnes and Samantha my love, Jones. And tell the fellas I say hello."

After I hang up, I cut open Hannah's envelope and something flutters out. It unfolds in its descent: a paper chain of snowflakes, each one white and crisp. There is no message inside. It's exactly what it appears to be.

chapter twenty-five

I SHOWED UP on the day of freshman orientation, accompanied by no one, a duffel over my shoulder stuffed with my clothes, some crackers, and the picture of Birdie. I saw Hannah's alarm when I appeared in our doorway. Then I saw her catch herself and smile.

She held out her hand, but her shock had taken me by the shoulders and shaken. I was here, at a school, surrounded by girls my own age. No one screamed at the television. No one stood for hours at their windows. No one avoided turning the tap for fear of ghosts.

I told myself, *Pull it together.*

I was a normal girl. I was not the kind to cause alarm. I was the kind who showered daily and wore clean clothes and answered the phone when it rang. When danger approached, I crossed the street. When mornings came, I ate breakfast.

This person who stood in the doorway wasn't me.

I shook Hannah's hand. I made my face smile.

"I must look like a disaster!" I said. "I've had a rough couple weeks. I'm going to set my stuff down and find the showers."

Did I see relief pass over her? I hoped so. I went to unzip my duffel but thought of all the dirty clothes stuffed inside, of the smell they'd emit, and thought better.

"I'm going to find the laundry, too," I said.

"Second floor," Hannah told me. "And the bathrooms are right around the corner. We did the family tour this morning."

I smiled again.

"Thanks," I said.

Most of the showers were in a row, locker-room style, but I found one full bathroom with a door that locked. I pulled off my shirt and my pants, let them drop to the floor. This place was so much cleaner than where I'd been.

I stepped out of my underwear, unclasped my bra. The girl in the mirror was feral. Puffy face, wild eyes, greasy hair. No wonder Hannah was shocked. I was shocked, too.

But I didn't have soap or shampoo. It was enough to make me cry. Water could only do so much.

I wanted a room full of steam and the smell of lavender or peach.

There was liquid soap on the wall by the sink. I pumped

as much as one hand could hold and then opened the shower door with the other. As if by magic, sitting on a shelf were containers of hotel shampoo, conditioner, and soap. I turned the tap and washed the yellow chemical soap down the drain. As the water warmed, I examined the little hotel bottles. Eucalyptus. I stepped under the water and closed myself into the square, mint-green-tiled space. Its smallness was comforting. All I heard was water falling, water echoing.

Eucalyptus filled the room.

I shampooed and rinsed until the bottle was empty. I washed my face and my body with the soap. I let the conditioner stay in for a very long time. In California, we were always worried about droughts, always conserving water. But I was far away.

"*I'm far away,*" I whispered.

I stayed longer. The hot water lasted forever. I knew I could wash away the dirt and the grease, but the wildness in my eyes was more difficult, and that was the worst part.

I told myself to just breathe.

I breathed in.

I breathed out.

Over and over. Until I wasn't aware I was in the shower, in the dorms, in New York. Until I wasn't aware of anything.

Putting dirty clothes back on was a sacrilege. I chose the least worn of them and stuffed the rest into the washer with detergent from the vending machine. Then I went to find the student store, desperate for something else to wear in the meantime.

The store was chaos. Parents and their kids swarmed through the aisles, admiring knickknacks, complaining over the cost of textbooks. The incoming freshmen whined and fretted; everything was the most important thing ever. I was invisible, moving silently among them toward the clothing section, the only solitary person there.

What I found filled me with awe.

I had no idea such school spirit could exist.

There were T-shirts and polo shirts and sweatshirts and sweatpants and shorts. Panties and boxers and bras. Pajamas and tank tops and socks and flip-flops. Even a dress! All of them emblazoned with the school colors and mascot. All of them so clean.

I bought an armful, over three hundred dollars' worth of clothes. As I swiped the ATM card, I tamped down the knowledge that my funds would run out. Not soon, but not too long from then either. Unless I found a way to start putting some money back in the account, I would be broke in a year.

I asked to use the dressing room on my way out and pulled on the clean bra and underwear. The panties had a picture of the mascot across the butt. They were fun, even if only I would ever see them. The bra was sportier than any I'd ever had, but it was cute anyway. The day was hot so I chose the terrycloth shorts, grateful that my blondness allowed me to show my legs even when I hadn't shaved them for a while. Last came a T-shirt, the creases still there from how it was folded.

I looked at myself in the full-length mirror.

My hair was clean and straight, still a little damp. My clothes fit me fine. I smelled like a spa. I looked like any other girl.

I stopped by the laundry room on the way back, but instead of putting my clothes in the dryer, I threw them into the trash.

Hannah was in her room when I showed up again, and this time her parents were there, too. Her mom was putting sheets on her bed. Her stepdad was hanging a framed poster from a Broadway production of *Rent*.

"Hi," I said from the doorway.

How many times do you get the chance to do something over again, to do it over right? You only get to make one first impression, unless the person you meet possesses a rare and specific kind of generosity. Not the kind that gives you the benefit of the doubt, not the kind that says, *Once I get to know her better she'll probably be fine,* but the kind that says, *No. Unacceptable.* The kind that says, *You can do better. Now show me.*

"You must be Marin!" her mom said. "We've been dying to meet you!"

"Now tell us," said her stepdad. "Is it Marin like mariner, or Marin like the county."

"The county," I said. "It's so nice to meet you."

I shook their hands.

Hannah said, "Nice to meet you, Marin." We smiled at each other as though the morning had never happened. "I hope you don't mind that I claimed this side."

"Not at all."

"Did your family leave already?" Hannah's mom asked.

"Actually, they couldn't make it. I'm getting started with this independence thing a little early."

Hannah's stepdad said, "Well, put us to work! We'd love to help."

"Do you have sheets?" her mom asked, folding Hannah's bedspread over.

I shook my head no. The bare mattress glared at me. I wondered how many other things I hadn't planned for.

"My mom packed me way too many sets," Hannah said.

"Well, good thing!" her mom said.

Soon Hannah's side of the room looked like she'd already lived there for months and mine was bare except for some red striped sheets, a soft pillow, and a cream-colored blanket.

"Thanks so much," I told her parents as they left. I tried to sound casually grateful and not how I really felt—as though they had saved my life.

And Hannah kept saving me. She saved me with never asking questions, with instead reading to me about bees and botany and evolution. She saved me with clothes she loaned me and never took back. She saved me with seats next to her in the dining hall, with quick evasions when people asked me questions I couldn't answer, with chapters read aloud and forced trips off campus and rides to the grocery store and a pair of winter boots.

chapter twenty-six

I TAKE A COUPLE PUSHPINS out of the jar on Hannah's desk and approach my empty bulletin board. I pin the snowflake chain along the top of it and then text Hannah a picture. She texts back right away, two high fives with a heart between them.

It feels so good. I want to do more. I take my new pot out of its bag and set it on my desk. My peperomia is thriving, each leaf full and luminous. Carefully, I ease its roots out of the plastic cup it came in. I pour the leftover dirt into Claudia's pot, and then place the roots in the middle, pressing the soil around it. I pour in some leftover water from a cup Mabel was using. I'll need to get more soil when I can, but it's enough for now.

I cross the room and turn to look at my desk. Two yellow

bowls, a pink pot with a green leafy plant, a strand of paper snowflakes.

It's pretty, but it needs something more.

I drag my desk chair over to my closet and stand on it so that I can reach the top shelf. I find the only thing up there: the photograph of my mother at twenty-two years old, standing in the sun. I borrow four of Hannah's silver push-pins and choose the right spot on my bulletin board, just to the right of the snowflakes, and push the pins in against the corners of the photograph so that they hold it up without making any holes. It's a big photograph, eight by ten prob-ably, and it transforms the corner.

I'm not saying that it doesn't scare me, to bring it into the light. My mother on Ocean Beach. Her sun-faded peach surfboard leaning under her arm. Her black wet suit and wet hair. Her squinting eyes and her huge smile.

It scares me, yes, but it also feels right.

I stare at her.

I try and I try and I try to remember.

A couple hours later, I take a long shower. I let the water run over me.

When I go back, whenever that will be, I'll need to find something of Gramps's to scatter or bury. I couldn't laugh at Jones's joke. Instead, it's echoing the way true things always do when I've been trying to deny them. *If your gramps had a grave, if your gramps had a grave.* Enough time has passed by now that I know Mabel is right. But another version of the story springs up sometimes, one of him with pockets full of a few thousand dollars, gambling winnings he kept for himself, on his way to the Rocky Mountains.

I need to give him a grave in order to contain him. I need to bury something to anchor his ghost. One of these days, in some not-so-far future, I'll take a trip into Jones's garage and I'll search through our old things and I'll assemble a box of objects instead of ashes and I'll find him a place to rest.

I rinse the conditioner out of my hair. I turn off the water and breathe in the steam.

He wore a gold chain around his neck on special occasions. I wonder if Jones bought it back for me.

I dry off and wrap myself in a towel. When I get back to my room, I look at my phone. It's only two o'clock.

I take a cue from the list I made on my first night here alone and make soup. I chop vegetables and boil pasta, pour a carton of chicken stock into a pot.

Once I've combined all the ingredients and it's time to wait while they cook, I turn to the second essay in the solitude book, but my mind is too full of different versions of the last summer's story. There's one where I fail him. Where I stop coming home so he stops making dinner, and I'm not around to see how much he needs me. And then there's one where he fails me. Where I feel it—that he doesn't want me there, that I'm in the way. So I stay away, for him and for me. So that I never face his rejection. So that I get to pretend I'm the most important thing to him, the way he is to me. Because if we have any sense of self-preservation, we do the best with what we're given.

I was given cakes and cookies and rides to school. I was given songs and dinners at a table with brass candlesticks. I was given a man with a sensitive heart and a devious sense of humor and enough skill at cards to win me a year of private college—tuition *and* room and board—and I took all of those good things and told myself they made us special. Told myself they meant we were a family the way Mabel and Ana and Javier were, told myself that we weren't missing anything.

We were masters of collusion, Gramps and I. In that, at least, we were together.

When yearbooks came out, I didn't flip straight to the back like everyone else to find the seniors' pages. Instead I started at the front. I looked through each page of freshman girls. I didn't even know them but I took my time, as though they were my friends. I studied the club pages, the sophomores, the sports teams. The juniors and the dances, the teachers and the theme days. Then the first senior page was upon me, and I read every quote, stared hard at the baby pictures of all of these girls. So many bows on bald heads, so many tiny dresses and tiny hands, so many pages to linger on before I got to mine.

As soon as I turned the page I saw myself.

Instead of leaving a blank space where my baby picture was meant to be, the editors made my senior portrait big enough to take up both spaces. All around me were my classmates as babies and then as their current selves; and then there I was, as though I had entered the world at eighteen in a black sleeveless blouse and a stiff smile. I thought I couldn't be the only one, but I got to the end, and I was. Even Jodi Price, adopted at eight, had a baby picture. Even Fen Xu, whose house had burned down the year before.

Those days and nights at the motel, I thought I was afraid of his ghost, but I wasn't.

I was afraid of my loneliness.

And how I'd been tricked.

And the way I'd convinced myself of so much: that I wasn't sad, that I wasn't alone.

I was afraid of the man who I'd loved, and how he had been a stranger.

I was afraid of how I hated him.

How I wanted him back.

Of what was in those boxes and what I might someday

discover and the chance I may have lost by leaving them behind.

I was afraid of the way we'd lived without opening doors.

I was afraid we had never been at home with each other.

I was afraid of the lies I'd told myself.

The lies he'd told me.

I was afraid that our legs under the table had meant nothing.

The folding of laundry had meant nothing.

The tea and the cakes and the songs—*all of it*—had meant nothing.

chapter twenty-seven

I AM AFRAID he never loved me.

chapter twenty-eight

THE WINTER SKY is bright gray and sharp. I see a bird come and go outside the window, a thin branch snap and drop.

I should have gone with her.

chapter twenty-nine

I'M SITTING ON TOP OF MY BED, leaning against the wall, watching the snow fall again. I want the thunder of ocean, a day that's cold but dry, the feeling that comes with heavy clouds in the distance. Relief from the drought. The novelty of being homebound. Wood in the fireplace, heat and light.

I didn't ask Jones what he meant when he said he kept the real stuff. If he meant my shells. Or the blue-and-gold blanket. Or the kitchen table with its collapsible leaves and the chairs that go with it. I try to imagine a future apartment. My own kitchen with decorations on the wall. Shelves with my collection of Claudia's pottery.

I don't know if I see the table and chairs and the blanket. I don't know if I want to.

If I keep looking out the window, I'll see the snow settle

on the paths again, cover the trees where hints of branches have started to show through.

I find a documentary online about an old woman who makes pottery every day from her home on a farm. I prop the computer on my desk chair and pull my blankets up and watch it. In ten days, it will be time to call Claudia. I hope she'll still want me. There are all of these close-up shots of the potter's hands in the clay. I can't wait to feel that.

My body is so still. This movie is so quiet. I want to swim, but I can't. It will be more than three weeks before everyone comes back and the pool is reopened and I feel that plunge, that rush. But I need to do *something*. Now. My limbs are begging me.

So I pause the movie and I stand up and go out in the hall. I take off my slippers and feel the carpet under my feet. I stare down the long, empty hallway, and then I'm running. I run until I'm at the very end, and then I run back, and I need something more, so this time, I open my mouth and my lungs and I yell as I run. I fill this designated historical building with my voice. And then I push open the door to the stairway and in here my voice echoes. I run to the top, not to take in the view but to feel myself moving, and I run and I yell and I run, until I've gone up and down each hallway of each floor. Until I'm panting and sweaty and satiated in some small but vital way.

I go back into my room and collapse on my bed. The sky is changing, becoming darker. I'm going to lie here, in this silent place, and stare out the window until the night turns black. I'll witness each color in the sky.

And I do. I feel peaceful.

But it's only five thirty, and there are ten more days until I can call Claudia, twenty-three more days until everyone comes back here.

I was okay just a moment ago. I will learn how to be okay again.

I turn the movie back on and watch until the end, and the credits roll and stop and the screen changes. There's a list of documentaries I might like. I hover over them to see what they're about, but I don't care enough to click on one. I lie back instead. I look at the dark ceiling and think about the door shutting between Mabel and me. She waved goodbye to me from inside the cab. Her boots were dry by then—we'd set them right next to the radiator and left them there all night—but they were blotchy and warped. I wonder if she'll put them in the trash when she gets home.

She should be arriving home around now. I get up to reach for my phone. If she texts me, I want to get her message right as it comes in. I want my reply to reach her right away. I lie back down with my phone next to me. I close my eyes and wait.

And then I hear something. A car. I open my eyes—light sweeps across the ceiling.

It must be Tommy, checking on me or the building. I flip on my light and step to the window to wave.

But it isn't a truck—it's a taxi—and it's stopping right here, in the circle in front of the entrance, and its doors are opening. All of its doors, all at once.

And I don't care that it's snowing; I throw open my window because there they are.

Mabel and Ana and Javier and the cab driver, opening the trunk.

"You're here?" I yell.

They look up and call hello. Ana blows me kiss after kiss. I race out of my room and down the stairs. I pause at the landing and look out the window because in the seconds that have passed I'm sure I must be imagining this. Mabel left for the airport this morning. She should be in San Francisco now. But they are still here, Mabel and Ana with suitcases next to their feet and bags slung over their shoulders, Javier and the driver wrestling a giant cardboard box from the trunk. I'm back in the stairwell going down, down, skipping steps. I might be flying. And then I'm in the lobby and they're approaching. The car is leaving, but they are still here.

"Are you mad?" Mabel asks. But I'm crying too hard to

answer. And I'm too full of happiness to be embarrassed that I made them do this.

"*Feliz Navidad!*" Javier says, leaning the box against the wall, opening his arms wide to embrace me, but Ana reaches me first, her strong arms pulling me close, and then they are all around me, all of them, arms everywhere, kisses covering my head and my cheeks, and I'm saying thank you, over and over, saying it so many times that I can't make myself stop until it's just Javier's arms left around me and he's whispering shhh in my ear, rubbing my back with his warm hand, saying, "Shhh, *mi cariño*, we are here now. We are here."

chapter thirty

ONCE WE'RE UPSTAIRS, we disperse, get to work. Mabel
leads them to the kitchen, and I follow behind, exhausted
but surrounded by light.

"The pots and pans are here," she says. "And here are
the utensils."

"Baking trays?" Ana asks.

"I'll look," Mabel says.

But I remember where they are. I open the drawer under
the oven.

"Here," I say.

"We need a blender for the mole," Javier says.

"I packed the immersion blender in my suitcase," Ana
tells him.

He sweeps her into his arms and kisses her.

"Girls," Ana says, still in his embrace. "Will you set up

the tree? We'll finish our grocery list and get the prep started. We have about an hour before the cab comes back."

"I found us a restaurant," Javier tells me. "A special Christmas Eve menu."

"What tree?" I ask.

Mabel points to the box.

We carry it into the elevator together and ride up to the rec room. We'll eat our Christmas dinner in there at the table, sit on the couches, and look at the tree.

"We can sleep in here," I say. "And give your parents my room."

"Perfect," she says.

We find a place for the tree by the window and open the box.

"Where did you get this?" I ask her, thinking of the tall pines they've always gotten and covered with hand-painted ornaments.

"It's our neighbor's," Mabel says. "On loan."

The tree comes in pieces. We stand up its middle section and then stick on the branches, longer pieces at the bottom and shorter as we build up, tier by tier. All white tinsel, all covered in lights.

"Moment of truth," Mabel says, and plugs it in. Hundreds of tiny bulbs glow bright. "It's actually really pretty."

I nod. I step back.

He would carry the boxes so carefully out to the living

room. Open their lids to tissue-paper-wrapped ornaments. Apple cider and sugar cookies. A pair of tiny angels, dangling between his finger and thumb as he searched for the right branch. Something catches in my chest. Breathing hurts.

"Jesus Christ," I whisper. *"Now, that's a tree."*

The restaurant is an Italian place, white tablecloths and servers in black ties. We are surrounded by families and laughter.

Ana chooses the wine, and the waiter comes back with the bottle.

"How many will be enjoying the Cabernet this evening?"

"All of us," Javier says, sweeping his arm across the table as though the four of us were a village, a country, the entire world.

"Wonderful," the waiter says, as though drinking laws don't exist during the holidays, or perhaps have never existed at all.

He pours wine into all of our glasses, and we order soups and salads and four different pastas, and no dish is spectacular but everything is good enough. Ana and Javier lead the conversation, full of gentle teasing of Mabel and one another, full of anecdotes and exuberance, and afterward we have a cab take us to Stop & Shop and wait as we race through the aisles, grabbing everything on the list. Javier curses the selection of cinnamon, saying they don't have the real stuff; and Ana drops a carton of eggs and they break with a tremendous *thwack* on the floor, yellow oozing out; but apart from that, we get everything they are looking for and ride, smushed in the cab with our groceries and the heat blasting, back to the dorm.

"Is there anything we can do to help?" I ask after we have gotten the bags of groceries unpacked in the kitchen.

"No," Javier says. "I have it under control."

"My dad is the boss tonight. My mom is the sous chef. Our job is to stay out of their way."

"Fair enough," I say. We step into the elevator but neither of us presses the number of my floor.

"Let's go to the top," I say.

The view must be the same as it was the first night we were up here, but it looks crisper and brighter, and even though we can't hear Ana and Javier as they chop and stir and laugh, I feel that we are less alone.

But maybe it doesn't have to do with Ana and Javier at all.

"When did you decide to do this?" I ask her.

"We thought you'd come home with me. That was our only plan. But when I realized that there was a good chance I wasn't going to convince you, we figured out that we could do this."

"Last night," I say. "When you were on the phone . . ."

She nods. "We were planning it out. They wanted me

to tell you, but I knew that if I did you might give in and go back before you were ready." She holds her hand up to the window. "We all understand. It makes sense why you don't want to go back yet."

She takes her hand away but the imprint is still there, a spot of warmth on the glass.

"When I was waiting for my parents at the airport, I kept thinking of something I wanted to ask you."

"Okay," I say.

She's quiet.

"Go ahead."

"I've just been wondering if there's anyone here you're interested in."

She's flushed and nervous, but trying to hide it.

"Oh," I say. "No. I haven't been thinking about things like that."

She looks disappointed, but slowly, her expression changes.

"Let's think about it now," she says. "There must be *someone* out there."

"You're doing it again," I say. "This is like the Courtney and Eleanor thing."

She shakes her head. "It's not like that. I just—it would make me feel better. It would make *you* feel better, too."

"I don't need to be with somebody in order for it to be okay that you have a boyfriend. It's okay already."

"Marin. I'm just asking you to think about it. I'm not saying you have to make some huge decision or fall in love or do anything that complicates your life."

"I'm fine as I am."

But she isn't backing down.

"Come on," she says. "*Think.*"

This is a New York college—it isn't Catholic school—and so many of the girls here wear little rainbow bracelets or pink triangle pins, so many of them talk casually about their ex-girlfriends or call the chair of the women's studies program hot. I've never joined in, but it's only because I don't talk about the things I left behind. But I've noticed, I guess, even though I've tried to close myself off. I've noticed a couple girls in spite of myself.

"You're thinking about someone," Mabel says.

"Not really."

"Tell me," she says.

I can see how much she wants this, but I don't want to do it. Even if there *was* someone, how could I keep telling myself that I'm fine with so little, that all I need is Hannah's friendship and the pool and scientific facts and my yellow bowls and a borrowed pair of winter boots, if I spoke a girl's name aloud? She'd become something I wished for.

"Is she pretty?"

It's too much coming from her mouth and the look in her eyes is too earnest and I'm too overwhelmed to answer.

I guess she needs this—for us to move on—but it feels like another loss. To think a new girl is pretty, and not in a way that lots of people in the world are pretty, but pretty in a way that might mean something to me. To look into Mabel's dark eyes, try not to stare at her pink mouth or her long hair, and say that. To think that a girl who is practically a stranger could be the next person I love. To think she might take Mabel's place.

But I think about Mabel's warmth on the pullout sofa. I think about her body against mine and I know that a lot of what I felt that night was about her, but that some of it wasn't. Maybe I am already hoping for that feeling again, with someone new. Maybe I just didn't know it.

Something in me is cracking open, the light coming through is so bright it hurts, and the rest of me is still here, wounded, even though I know it's all for the best.

"That night at the beach," Mabel says. "And the days after, until school ended and all through the summer . . ."

"Yeah?"

"I thought I'd never love another person."

"I thought that, too."

"I guess we should have known better."

"I don't know about that," I say.

I close my eyes. Here we are on Ocean Beach. Here's the whiskey bottle in the sand and the sound of waves crashing and the cold wind and the darkness and Mabel's smile against my collarbone. Here we are in that spectacular summer. We are different people now, yes, but those girls were magic.

"I'm glad we didn't know better," I say.

"I guess you're right. It would have been simpler, but you know . . ."

Our eyes meet. We smile.

"Should we watch a movie or something?"

"Yes," I say.

We take a last look out of the window at the night, and I send a silent wish to everyone out there for this kind of warmth. Then we are in the elevator. The mahogany walls, the chandelier. The doors shut us in and we begin the descent. And when they open again we are in the rec room, standing before a tinsel tree, glowing and white. It's nothing like Gramps's firs, but it's perfect in its own way.

"Whoever she is, maybe I'll meet her someday," Mabel says.

"Maybe someday."

I say it with so much uncertainty, but who knows, I guess. *Someday* is an open word. It could mean tomorrow or it could be decades away. If someone had told me while I was huddled under the motel blankets that Mabel and I would be together again someday, that I would tell her the story of what happened someday and feel a little better, a little less afraid, I wouldn't have believed it. And it's only been four months since then, which is not long to wait for someday.

I don't say that maybe I'll meet Jacob, even though I know that I should. It's more likely and more imminent. But I can't say it yet.

"Look." Mabel's in front of the TV, sorting through the movie choices. "It's *Jane Eyre*. Have you seen this one?"

I shake my head. I've only seen the black-and-white version.

"What do you think? In honor of our night without electricity?" I hesitate, and she says, "Or we can go with something lighter."

But why not? The story's been on my mind, and I know it so well already. There will be no surprises, so I say yes.

It begins with Jane as a young woman, rushing from Thornfield, crying. Another shot, she's alone against a bleak landscape. A sky on fire, thunder, rain. She thinks she's going to die. And then the film goes back in time and she's a little girl and we're learning how everything started.

Gramps set up that tree every year. He pulled out the decorations his dead wife and dead daughter bought and pretended to be a man who had lost too much and survived it. He pretended, for me, that his mind and his heart were not dark and convoluted places. He pretended that he lived in a house with me, his granddaughter, for whom he baked and often drove to school and taught important lessons about how to treat stains and save money, when really he lived in a secret room with the dead.

Or maybe not. Maybe it's more complicated.

There are degrees of obsession, of awareness, of grief, of insanity. Those days and nights in the motel room I weighed each of them against the other. I tried to make sense of what had happened, but each time I came up short. Each time I thought I may have understood, some line of logic snapped and I was thrust back into not knowing.

It's a dark place, not knowing.

It's difficult to surrender to.

But I guess it's where we live most of the time. I guess it's where we *all* live, so maybe it doesn't have to be so lonely. Maybe I can settle into it, cozy up to it, make a home inside uncertainty.

Jane is at her cruel aunt's deathbed now. She's forgiving her and returning home. And here is Mr. Rochester, waiting for her, in all his Byronic heroism. She isn't sure if she should trust him or fear him. The answer is both. There's so much he hasn't told her yet. There's that wife of his, locked up in the attic. There are so many lies of omission. There's the trick he's going to play on her, the way he'll pretend to be somebody else and snake his way into her heart. He'll scare her. She'll be right to be afraid.

There's so much I could have found out if I'd gone home

after the police station. I could have kept windows shut tight so that his ghost couldn't get in and torn through all of my mother's things. I could have touched every photograph. I could have combed his letters for clues about her. There must have been hints of the past in there, woven in with Gramps's dreams of her life in Colorado. There would have been so much about her to discover, even if half of it wasn't true.

"Here it comes," Mabel says.

I feel it, too, getting closer—the proposal. First anguish and then love. Rochester doesn't deserve her, but he loves her. He means what he says, but he's a liar. I hope that this movie will keep the words as Brontë wrote them. They're so beautiful. And yes—here they are.

"'I have a strange feeling with regard to you. As if I had a string somewhere under my left ribs, tightly knotted to a similar string in you. And if you were to leave I'm afraid that cord of communion would snap. And then I've a notion that I'd take to bleeding inwardly.'"

"Like the vein in *The Two Fridas*," Mabel whispers.

"Yeah."

Jane says, "'I am a free human being with an independent will, which I now exert to leave you.'"

And maybe she should go through with it, maybe she *should* leave. We already know it would spare her some heartache. But it feels so much better right now to say yes, to stay, and Mabel and I are swept up in it. For a little while, it takes me outside of myself. For a few minutes, Jane believes that she'll be happy, and I try to believe it, too.

Near the end of the movie, Ana and Javier come into the room, wrapped gifts in their arms. They set them under the tree and watch with us as Jane walks through the wreckage of Thornfield to find Rochester again.

They leave when the credits roll and then come back with a few more gifts.

"Is the package still in your bag?" I ask Mabel.

She nods and I find it. It looks unfinished against the festive wrapping paper of the presents they brought, but I'm glad to have something for them. I realize now why Mabel tried to wait to open hers and I'm sad that I don't have something else to give her.

Javier laughs at the white tree. He shakes his head.

Ana shrugs. "It's kitsch. It's fun."

Quiet descends. I can feel how late it is.

"Mabel," Javier says. "Can you come with me for a moment?" and soon it's only Ana and me on the sofa next to the glittering lights. And when Ana turns to me, I realize that our solitude has been orchestrated.

She says, "I have something I want to tell you."

Her mascara has smudged under her eyes, but she doesn't look tired.

"May I?" she asks, and takes my hand. I squeeze hers back, expect her to let go but she doesn't.

She says, "I wanted to be your mother. From the first night I met you, I wanted that."

Everything in me begins to buzz. My scalp and my fingers and my heart.

"You came into the kitchen with Mabel. You were fourteen. I already knew a couple things about you, my daughter's new friend whose name was Marin, who lived alone with her grandfather, who loved reading novels and talking about them. I watched you look around. You touched the painted dove above the sink when you thought no one was looking."

"I don't like to anymore," I find myself saying.

She looks confused.

"Read novels," I say.

"You probably will again. But even if you don't, it doesn't matter."

"But what if it does?"

"What do you mean?"

"What if I'm not that girl who walked into your kitchen?"

"Ah," she says. "Okay. I see."

The heater rattles; the hot air blows. She leans back to think, but still holds my hand tight.

I'm making this hard for her. All I want is to say yes.

"Mabel told us everything. About the two of you. About Gramps and how he died. About what you discovered after he was gone." Tears fill her eyes and spill over but she hardly seems to notice. "Tragedy," she says. "Heartbreak." She stops and then she makes sure that I'm looking at her. "*Betrayal*." Her eyes bore into mine. "Understand?"

They had waited for me in the station lobby and I left through the back exit. I didn't call them back a single time. I made Mabel come here to track me down, and now I've made them come to me as well.

"I'm so sorry," I say.

"No, no," she says, as though I've asked to wear lingerie to a school dance. "Not us, you. *You* were betrayed," she says.

"Oh."

"These are all things that change a person. If we endure them and we aren't changed, then something is wrong. But do you remember her? That dove in my kitchen?"

"Of course," I say. I think of how beautifully painted her head is. I think of her copper wings.

"You are still you," Ana says. "And I still want to be your mother. You were alone for longer than you realized. He did the best he could. I am certain of that. He loved you. There is no question. But since that night when you called Javier and me for help, we have been waiting for a time to tell you that we want you in our family. We would have told you that morning, but you weren't ready."

She wipes tears off my face but more rush after.

"Say yes," she says.

She presses her mouth to my cheek, and my heart swells, my chest aches.

"Say yes."

She smooths my hair behind my ear, away from my wet face. I can't stop crying. This is more than a room with my name on a door. More than glasses of water out of their kitchen sink.

She pulls me close to her, until I'm smaller than I knew I could be. Until I fit against her chest, my head nestled where her neck meets her shoulder, and I gasp because I remember something.

I thought that Ocean Beach would do it or maybe the pink shells or the staring at her photograph. I thought that one of these things, one day, might help me remember.

But it happens now, instead.

My mother's salty hair, her strong arms, her lips against the top of my head. Not the sound of her voice, not her words, but the feeling of her singing, the vibrations of her throat against my face.

"Say yes," Ana says.

My tiny hand clutching a yellow shirt.

The sand and the sun.

Her hair like a curtain, keeping me shaded.

Her smile when she looked at me, burning with love.

It's all I remember, and it's everything.

I'm still gasping. I'm holding Ana tight. If she lets go, the memory might go with her. But she holds me close for a very long time, and then she takes my face between her hands and says, "Say yes."

The memory is still here. I can still feel it.

And I have yet another chance, and I take it.

"Yes," I say. "Yes."

We were on a beach and the sun was bright and I was in my mother's arms. She was singing to me. I can't hear the song, but I can hear the tone of her voice; and when the singing stopped, she rested her face on my head. The whole world was out there. Honeybees and deciduous trees. Swimming pools and grocery stores. Men with vacant eyes, bells on diner doors, motels so bleak and lonely they settle in your bones. Mabel and Ana and the man Gramps would become or perhaps was already. Each someday and each kiss. Each specific kind of heartbreak. The whole world was out there, but I was in my mother's arms, and I didn't know it yet.

acknowledgments

A few months after my grandfather died, in a time when I cried at every thought of him, my wife, Kristyn, said, *I have a story idea for you. What if you write about a girl who lives near Ocean Beach with her grandfather?* The idea stayed with me. On the one-year anniversary of his death, our daughter, Juliet, was born. Then, in the early summer when she was an infant, I took a walk by myself to our local café and suddenly the voices of Marin, Mabel, and Gramps all came to me in snippets of dialogue and Marin's broken longing. I think Kristyn had a different kind of story in mind, because the love my grandfather and I shared was uncomplicated, and with the exception of his penchant for cracking jokes and playing cards, he had little in common with Gramps. But I wrote the novel during a time of upheaval and disillusionment that was in stark contrast to the aching and magical love of our new family, and this book is the culmination of all of that. Kristyn, thank you for the seeds of this story, and for your fierce and unwavering love. And to my kind and curious and wild Juliet, thank you for making me the person who could write this novel.

I send heartfelt thanks to my writing group—Laura Davis, Teresa Miller, and Carly Anne West—who assured me from the beginning that, despite my fears, this book didn't consist only of making food and washing bowls. Thank you to Jules LaCour for his help with the Spanish and Adi Alsaid for sharing his cultural knowledge. Thank you to Jessica Jacobs, my original critique partner, for the invaluable final read, and to Amanda Krampf for the thousands of conversations along the way.

To my Penguin family, by the time this novel comes out, it will be ten glorious years that we've been together. Thank you to Julie Strauss-Gabel for, among many other things, the gift of that long discussion over lunch in San Francisco, during which you helped me (yet again) to unearth the heart of my story and to believe it was enough. Here's to many more books together. My huge and everlasting gratitude to the Dutton team: Melissa Faulner, Rosanne Lauer, Anna Booth, and Anne Heausler; the designers who gave this story such a beautiful package: Samira Iravani and Theresa Evangelista; and my incredible publicist Elyse Marshall. And thank you to all of you who, now that this book is finished, are making sure it finds a place in bookstores and libraries and schools and the Internet. You make magic.

Sara Crowe, I'm so fortunate to have you by my side. Thank you for all you do.

Finally, to my family and friends, I'm grateful for each one of you.

Questions for Discussion

1. What does the title phrase, "We are okay," mean to you? What does it mean for Marin to be okay? How does that evolve over the course of the novel?

2. Marin feels a profound sense of loneliness when *We Are Okay* begins. How is it possible to be "alone even when surrounded by people"?

3. We learn that Gramps also struggled with loneliness. How is Marin's loneliness different from her grandfather's?

4. Settings (time, place, season, weather, mood), and the contrast between California and New York, are very important in *We Are Okay*. How are the settings symbolic of the person that Marin was and is, and her life in each of these places?

5. Rather than following a linear timeline, LaCour switches back and forth between the present and the past throughout the novel. How does this affect the movement of the story? How does it impact you as a reader?

6. A recurring theme in *We Are Okay* has to do with both figurative and literal ghosts. How does each character deal with their own ghosts? What are the consequences of those choices?

7. Why do you think Marin's personal loss changes the way she reads and analyzes literature? How can life shift the way we experience books? How can books shift the way we experience life?

8. Grief is a palpable emotion in *We Are Okay*. How do the different characters manage their own grief? How did the book impact the way you understand grief?

turn the page for a preview of
Nina LaCour's new novel,
Watch Over Me.

had we been telling the truth

ON THE MORNING OF MY INTERVIEW I slept until eight, went downstairs to the kitchen, and poured myself the last of the coffee. I stood at the counter, watching out the window as I sipped, and then pushed up my sleeves and turned on the water to wash the breakfast dishes that Amy and Jonathan had left stacked in the sink.

In just a few days, I would leave them.

Amy had bought a crib and tucked it into the garage. A few days after that, she came home with a bag from a toy store. A stuffed bunny peeked over the side. She asked me how my English final went and I told her that I wrote about the collapse of social mores in a couple of short stories and she said it sounded great. And then she took the bag into their bedroom as though it were nothing.

She was only being kind. I knew that. They hadn't asked me to stay.

The sink was empty. I scrubbed it until it was perfectly white and then I turned off the water. I tried to breathe. I tried not to want this so badly.

My phone buzzed.

"Are you ready?" Karen asked. She'd been my social worker for four years and even though I could tell she was in traffic, probably dribbling coffee on her skirt and checking her email as she talked to me, she calmed my racing heart.

"I think so," I said.

"Remember—they read your letter. I've told them so much about you. They've talked to all your references. This is just a final step. And you get to make sure you really want it."

"I want it."

"I know you do, honey. I want it for you too. Call me as soon as it's over."

He knocked at ten thirty, exactly when he said he'd arrive.

"Mila?" he asked when I opened the door. He stuck out his hand. "Nick Bancroft. So nice to finally meet you."

I led him into the kitchen, where a round table sat beneath a window in the sun and the chairs were close enough for friendly conversation but far enough apart for strangers.

"How are you doing?" he asked after we sat.

"Well, finals are over, so that's good," I said.

"Yes, congratulations. Your transcripts are solid. Have you considered college?"

I shrugged. "Maybe I'll go at some point."

He nodded, but I saw that he felt sorry for me. My eyes darted to the window. I didn't know how to talk about my life with someone who understood. I clenched a fist in my lap and forced myself not to cry. I was ready to prove my work ethic, talk about the hours I spent volunteering at the library, and assure him that I was not afraid of dirt or messes or children throwing tantrums—but I was not ready for this.

"So, let me tell you about Terry and Julia and the farm," he said, taking mercy on me. "They adopted me when I was three, so it's been home basically all my life. I haven't lived at the farm in a long time, but I help them run the finances and I do all the interviews." I felt my fist unclench and I settled into the chair and listened to him tell me about the things I had already learned from talking to Karen and reading a *San Francisco Chronicle* article from fifteen years ago with the headline MENDOCINO COUPLE ADOPTS FORTIETH FOSTER CHILD. He talked about the farm and how everyone contributes to running it, from the children to the interns, and how as an intern I would spend my weekdays teaching in the schoolhouse and my Sundays waking up at five a.m. to run the booth at the farmers' market. He told me about the holidays when all the grown-up children come back to visit. "It becomes home if you let it," he said. "Even for the interns. I know that might sound hard to believe, but it's true."

"When do I find out?"

"Oh!" he said. "I thought you knew. You've been chosen already. It's yours if you want it."

My hands flew to my face. "Thank you," I said. And then I couldn't say anything else. He nodded, that look of sympathy again, and kept talking.

"Most of your hours will be spent in the school. They've

designed a curriculum and your job will be to learn it and teach the six- to nine-year-olds. There is only one of them right now, I think, but more will come soon. And Terry and Julia will be there to help."

"Would you like some tea?" I blurted. I had meant to ask him when he got there but had been too nervous. Now that I knew I was chosen, I wanted him to stay and tell me every-thing. Maybe that way I could hold it inside me—a real, live thing—in the days between that one and the one of my arrival.

"Sure," he said. I filled the kettle and set some boxes in front of him. He chose peppermint, and as I poured the steam-ing water over the leaves I breathed in the scent and it was like starting over already.

"I want to make sure you understand what this is," Nick said. "Quite a few people have turned it down. And some people haven't known what they were getting into and it hasn't worked out. You need to *want* it. It's a farm. It's in the middle of nowhere—to one side is the ocean and in every other direction is nothing but rocky hills and open land. It's almost always foggy and cold and there's no cell service and no town to shop in or meet people—Mendocino is forty-five minutes away. Farmers'-market days are the only times you'll interact with the outside world, and you'll be weigh-ing squashes and wrapping flowers most of the time."

"That's fine," I said. "I don't mind."

He warned me that the cabins where the interns live were tiny, only one room with wood-burning stoves for heat. He said that there was a landline but no cell service, and that everyone ate meals together three times a day and took turns with prep and cleanup.

"The main house is comfortable and you're always welcome in it. They have tons of books and a bunch of instruments. There's even a grand piano in the living room."

"I've always wanted to play the piano," I said. I don't know why I didn't tell him about all my years of lessons and the songs I knew by heart. "Someone to Watch Over Me" began to play in my brain, and the kitchen filled with music. My grandmother was sitting next to me, her fingers showing me where my fingers should go. Nick kept talking, and I listened over the sound of piano notes, full and rising. I had been so young. I didn't tell him about the terrible thing I'd done. He didn't ask those kinds of questions. Funny, when interviewing for a job to work with children, that a person would ask about college and remoteness and not say, *Tell me the worst thing you ever did. Tell me about your wounds. Can I trust you?*

Had they known the truth about me they might not have given me the job, I thought, even though I was determined to be good. Even though I held on fiercely to my own goodness.

By the time he finished his tea, we had it all planned out. He asked if I wanted to wait until after the graduation ceremony and I said no, that I didn't care about wearing a hat and robe and walking with the other students. Okay, he said, then he would pick me up on Sunday and we would drive up together. He gave me a thin volume called *Teaching School: A*

Handbook to Education on The Farm and asked me to read it. He said, "Mila, I have a good feeling about this. I think you'll be a perfect fit with all of us." And I told him I had a good feeling about it, too. And I told him that I felt lucky, and he said, "You *are* lucky. We all are."

And then he left.

———————

Had we been telling the truth, he would have said, *The place where I'm sending you—it looks beautiful, but it's haunted.*

Okay, I would have said.

It will bring everything back. All that you tried to bury.

I understand.

It's going make you want to do bad things.

I have experience with that.

And how did it turn out?

Terribly. But I promise to do better next time.

We could have had that conversation—it would not have been impossible. I would not have told him everything about me, but I would have told him enough. I still would have taken that four-hour drive up the jagged coastline to be with Terry and Julia and Billy and Liz and Lee and the rest of the children. All I'm saying is it would have been easier had I known.

Nina LaCour is the author of the widely acclaimed *Hold Still*, *The Disenchantments*, *Everything Leads to You*, and the Michael L. Printz Award–winning novel *We Are Okay*. She is also the coauthor, with David Levithan, of *You Know Me Well*. Formerly a bookseller and high school English teacher, she is now a faculty member of Hamline University's MFA in Writing for Children and Young Adults. A San Francisco Bay Area native, Nina lives with her family in Martinez, California. **www.ninalacour.com**

With a foreword by Nicola ~~Yoon~~, #1 *New York Times* bestselling author of *~~The Sun Is Also a Star~~* and *Everything, Everything*

National Bestseller & **Winner of the Michael L. Printz Award**

"Poetic and gorgeously written." —*The New York Times Book Review*

"A tender and beautiful exploration of grief and the freeing power of truth." —*Entertainment Weekly*

"A beautiful, devastating piece of art." —*BookPage*

You go through life thinking there's so much you need . . . Until you leave with only your phone, your wallet, and a picture of your mother.

Marin hasn't spoken to anyone from her old life since the day she left everything behind. No one knows the truth about those final weeks and the tragedy Marin has tried to outrun. Not even her best friend, Mabel. Now, months later, alone in an emptied dorm for winter break, Marin waits. Mabel is coming to visit and Marin will finally be forced to face everything that's been left unsaid and confront the loneliness that has made a home in her heart.

An intimate whisper that packs an indelible punch, this gorgeously crafted and achingly honest portrayal of grief will leave you urgent to reach across any distance to reconnect with the people you love.

COVER ART © 2017 BY ADAMS CARVALHO
COVER DESIGN BY SAMIRA IRAVANI
penguinrandomhouse.com

PENGUIN BOOKS   USA $11.99 | CAN $16.49
ISBN 978-0-14-242293-9

9 780142 422939

51199